Delta Heat

Patricia S. Jackson

Copyright © 2024 by Patricia S. Jackson
ISBN: 978-1-77883-427-1 (Paperback)

All rights reserved. No part of this publication may be reproduced, distributed, or transmitted in any form or by any means, including photocopying, recording, or other electronic or mechanical methods, without the prior written permission of the publisher, except in the case brief quotations embodied in critical reviews and other noncommercial uses permitted by copyright law.

The views expressed in this book are solely those of the author and do not necessarily reflect the views of the publisher, and the publisher hereby disclaims any responsibility for them.

BookSide Press
877-741-8091
www.booksidepress.com
orders@booksidepress.com

Contents

Delta Heat 4
PROLOGUE 6
   CHAPTER ONE 12
   CHAPTER TWO 23
   CHAPTER THREE 33
   CHAPTER FOUR 41
   CHAPTER FIVE 49
   CHAPTER SIX 54
   CHAPTER SEVEN 63
   CHAPTER EIGHT 72
   CHAPTER NINE 80
   CHAPTER TEN 87
   CHAPTER ELEVEN 96
   CHAPTER TWELVE 106
   CHAPTER THIRTEEN 113
About the Author 119

Delta Heat

He wanted to smell her, touch her, just simply be near her. There was an outside force so strong that he just had to follow up on it.

Once the hot water soothed his body, he decided to dress in something cool and relaxing before he went to Reba's house and visit Milya's room.

The weather was extremely hot and muggy, sort of sticky like. The Delta was known for its heat during the summer months. He put on a t-shirt and a pair of cut-off blue jeans. Lacing up his running shoes, he left Uncle Bennie's house to find comfort in Milya's room.

As he stepped out of the house, a thought quickly entered his mind. It worked once, maybe it will work again. He decided to enter her room again through the window. He was not ready to face anyone just yet. Why entering the house couldn't be done the correct way he didn't know. Hem wanted this time to be his, and his alone.

He reached her window and pushed it lightly. It moved with ease just as it did the first time. She was there before when he tried this, maybe she'll be there this time too.

Hoping against all odds, Rick crawled through the window and stopped once he made it on the inside. He looked outside to see if anyone saw him. Turning around, he stopped dead in his tracks. It was like seeing a mirage.

Patricia S. Jackson

To Bessie L. Franklin, Sharon W. Walker, Kyshea W. Nicholas, Albetha Williams, Demitria Hobbs, Eva Hudson, Shontice Cage, Angela P. Jones, Debra C. Paige, and The Queens.
This book is also dedicated to everyone who provided inspiration and support. Special thanks to my mother, Bessie F. Simmons, to Wyzene Gilleylen, Katrina Williams, Walter Allen III, and to the cornerstones of my life, my husband and children, Jerry, Carmilya, and Jerry Jr.

PROLOGUE

Life in the city can be competitive as well as strenuous. Something as simple as buying groceries in the best markets available could test your skill, just as competition can in the workplace. Milya found that out the moment she moved to New York City and began living in the fast lane. You had to have stamina, courage and confidence to survive in the "Big Apple, " and Milya had all of the above.

Sitting at a table with a few co-workers during the lunch hour, Milya Hargrove discussed upcoming business and social events that had been scheduled for the year.

One of the guys at the table said, "You've had a great morning Milya, business has been good for you today."

"Yeah, that's why I'm taking off this afternoon."

"Taking off to do what? Never mind, don't answer that. By the way, when are you going to introduce me to this friend of yours?"

"Who? Zaria."

"She's the one you've told me about for months, isn't she?"

"She'll be in on a flight this afternoon. As a matter of fact, I should be leaving now in order to make it to the airport on time. I'll see you guys at the party later. Don't worry, she'll be with me."

"Hey, before you leave, can you do me a favor?"

"What's that?"

"Wink your eye at that guy sitting across from us. He's been sopping you up as if you were a biscuit with gravy ever since we've been here.

Milya turned slowly and saw several attractive men seated at the table in question, but one particularly stood out. She'd seen him several times before, she just couldn't place him.

"Which One?" she asked.

"Never mind, just leave and pick up your friend. Make sure you bring back my enchanted gift."

"Bye."

Milya excused herself, picked up her purse and left the restaurant. She had a walk of distinction about her, and people automatically looked in her direction when she passed by. She had a certain flare that exuded self-confidence.

Zaria's flight made it without any mishaps, and arrived on time. Milya was waiting at the gate when Zaria got off the plane.

"Hi girl," Milya said as they embraced each other in a sisterly hug. "Boy do I have plans for you. We have a busy schedule."

"Well then, don't just stand there, help me with my luggage so we can go."

"My GOD girl, what didn't you bring?" "Well, I wasn't sure what to include, so I brought a little of this and a little of that."

They left the airport and drove the short distance to her home. When they arrived, Milya made sure that Zaria got settled in. She had received an invitation earlier in the week to a dinner party and wanted Zaria to attend the special event with her. She surely hoped Zaria felt up to going.

The dinner would be held at Congressman Jay Williams and his wife's home, which was the center of entertainment. She had gone there once or twice before for different gatherings. They shared a beautiful home.

"What's on the agenda for tonight?" Zaria asked.

"Are you interested in going to a dinner party?"

"Yes girl. I'm ready for anything.

Hey, I see that sparkle in your eyes.

Don't get that crazy notion you always have of trying to hook a sister up with someone.

"I'm not interested. I'm here to relax and have a great time. That's my main reason for taking off. Okay?" Zaria said as she gave Milya that all too knowing look.

"Whatever you say."

The party was in full swing when they arrived. Although it was a chilly night out, people were mingling on the grounds of the house as well as inside. Congressman Williams and his wife greeted them as they entered their home. Milya saw a few people she knew, and of-course Alonzo Ward was there waiting to meet Zaria.

She approached him with Zaria by her side. "Hi Alonzo, this is my best friend Zaria Monroe. Zaria, this is a co-worker of mine, Alonzo Ward." They exchanged pleasantries. Alonzo was not a good looking man, but he was handsome, and had a sturdy build. In Zaria's book, that was workable.

Just as Zaria and Alonzo started to engage in conversation, Milya turned away, and left the two of them standing there. She didn't have to look around to know that Zaria was shooting daggers into her back with her eyes.

Milya looked down at her feet, because she felt something slippery. She was not paying attention to where she was going, when she bumped into something hard and solid.

"Pardon me," she said even before she looked up to see who it was.

"It's ok," a deep voice replied. "Are you alright?" He asked.

She then looked at the person to whom the sexy voice belonged. "GOD, it's him," she thought.

"Yes I'm fine, did I injure you?" she asked smiling up at him.

"No you didn't, but I could be persuaded to let you hurt me," he countered.

"Oh could you now? And your name is?" She questioned.

"Rick, Rick Cantello."

"Hi Rick, it's nice to meet you," she said as she turned her back and walked away.

He was not to be out done, so he caught up with her and continued to chat for a while. She was more interested in finding Zaria and Alonzo. When she found them, the four of them continued to hangout together the rest of the night and they actually enjoyed the evening.

They naturally clicked and found pleasure in each other's company, after an elusive game of hide and seek. Milya thought that she had definitely met "Mr. Right" , the man of her dreams. Over the course of time, she had introduced him to her family and friends.

One winter's evening while attending a party, Rick introduced Milya to a few of his shady friends. Since he was occupied for the moment, she decided to go to the ladies room and freshen up a bit. Once conversation between two female friends. "Hey Melody, did you see Rick Cantello and his mechanical doll tonight?"

"Yeah girl, I saw them, and I'm wondering if she knows about his other friend."

"You mean his friends, don't you?"

"Well yes, but I'm thinking of one friend in particular."

"Oh her. What is she, about seven or eight months pregnant now?"

"Probably, and I hear she's not the only one that he has with child."

"Hell, I'd love to be knocked up by him too."

The two of them laughed as they continued to discuss him while leaving the restroom.

At first, Milya nearly went into shock.

Then she immediately saw fire. How dare he not inform her of his situation. A child or children was possibly involved.

She took a deep breath and composed herself, and then went in search of him.

He was still where she left him, sitting at the bar. She walked up to him and touched him lightly on his arm. He turned then and smiled at her, placing his hand over hers.

"I'm not feeling very well, can we leave now?" Milya asked gazing into his eyes.

Because what she had to say and discuss with him would definitely have to be said in private.

"Sure darling, " he said, then told most of the people goodnight.

They rode back to his place in silence.

Rick was wondering what was going on, but he decided to let her make the first move.

Once inside the condo, Milya said, "Well Rick, I've just heard some disturbing news and to be frank with you, I want to know if there's any truth to it." She turned toward him and asked, "Are you an expectant father?"

The question surprised him and made him furious, but his face remained unreadable.

"Milya," he said, "where did you hear something like that?" as he spoke in a tone that neither denied nor confirmed the accusation.

"Does it matter? The fact remains the same, you didn't mention it to me. Is someone expecting your child?"

"That's what I've been told." he said matter-of-factly, while trying to contain his own temper. "The child is not mine. I do not have any children anywhere. Is there anything else you would like to discuss?" He asked her calmly.

"Yes as a matter of fact there is. Let me lay it on the line for you. I will not have you playing me along with anyone else."

He cut her off by saying, "Milya, I'm not involved with anyone else. How long have we been together?" Before she could answer he went on rambling. "Have I ever given you cause to doubt me? Have I ever been disrespectful to you? The answer is no! So why are you questioning me now over something you heard?"

"Because you didn't deny it when I asked." she yelled. "I don't know what you're doing when you're not with me. I don't have the time nor the energy to keep up with you. The point is, in your spare time, you should be thinking of ways to enhance our relationship."

"That is something that I always think about. You are very important to me."

"Rick, tell me this, have you been intimately involved with the female in question?"

Rick's jaws twitched, that was the only indication that he was disturbed by this line of questioning. "Yes Milya, I have, but it's not like you think."

The debate went on for what seems like hours with no one giving an inch. He kept insisting that the child was not his.

Milya had had just about all she could stand. This shouting match was not solving anything. It was time to draw the line.

"Wait!" Milya Hargrove said, more sternly than she intended to sound. Taking a deep breath, "I'm tired of trying to reason with you Rick, (holding his seething gaze), we've been over this too many times."

Thinking to herself, Milya knew that tonight would be the last time she would probably ever see Rick again. She was not ready to deal with deceit.

Rick Cantello was a jack of all trades.

He had a lot of irons in the fire. He was a well-known realtor, businessman and handyman all wrapped up in one. His family was in the oil business in Texas, and proceeds were good from it.

Rick stood about five feet eleven and one half inches. He was really something to see. Closing her eyes, she envisioned his skin color which reminded her of the richness of caramel candy.

Interrupting her thoughts, Rick said, "Dammit Milya! ", either we talk now, straighten things out, or we don't talk at all."

Sensing that his temper was on the verge of exploding as well as her own, Milya turned, picked up her coat and purse, and walked out of his condo.

CHAPTER ONE

Startled from her sleep, Milya awoke with a feeling that something was wrong. She attempted to lie still and get her bearings, wondering if something was in her apartment. But all she could sense, lying in her bed in the dark, were the regular noises of the night.

The air conditioner had just kicked on and she could feel the low breeze from the ceiling fan.

Thinking back now, she tried to remember if she had dreamt of something that would have caused her to jump in her sleep.

For some reason, her mind was drawing a blank... Lost in thought, she could not recall dreaming at all when suddenly she heard that noise again.

She cringed at the thought that something or even someone may be in her apartment.

Sitting erect, almost tumbling out of her bed, Milya waited.... trying to figure out what and where the noise may or may not be coming from.

She had once been told, "If you thought that you may not be home alone, sit still with your weapon at hand and wait. You would have a better chance of seeing the intruder before he sees you, and the element of surprise can be a great advantage."

As that thought leaped from her mind, she no longer heard anything.

Total silence greeted her. This was spookier by the minute.

A thousand things crossed her mind, but there was no time to react because the noise was there again.

Milya could not take it any longer. She had to investigate the direction from which she thought the noise had come, and that was the kitchen, so she would start there first.

She grabbed her baseball bat that she kept under the bed, and moved lightly through the apartment.

As she moved along the hallway trying not to brush against the pictures hanging on wall. She thought to herself.

Milya was originally from the Delta in Mississippi. She returned to teach a small class at one of the local colleges, and the summer session was just about to begin, but could not end quickly enough for her.

She was doing this as a favor for one of her friends.

"Never again," she was thinking when the noise brought her attention back to the matter at hand.

She knew at that point that she was definitely not at home alone. Gathering her courage, Milya jumped into the kitchen swinging the bat in her hands with full force, when something ran past her at the speed of light.

Screaming!, she immediately turned on the lights, to find a dark brown and beige cat poised for a fight.

If she had been thinking clearly, she would have laughed at the situation, but she was horrified.

She didn't like cats, didn't like the way their tails curled around your legs and didn't like the pleading look in their eyes.

"Get Out!" she yelled, as if the cat understood and could just walk to the door, open it and walk out. How did it get inside she wondered? Looking around the room, she noticed that the kitchen window was open. She could have sworn she closed and locked everything when she moved in, but apparently she had not.

Calming down a little, after figuring it must have been the cat who was making the noises, she walked to the back door and let the cat out.

As soon as she opened the door, the cat ran out as if something was after it. Peering out into the darkness of the night, Milya thought she saw a shadow. But upon closing her eyes for a brief moment to adjust her vision to the unilluminated sky, there was nothing to be seen.

Second guessing herself, Milya locked the door and window securely. Walking to the refrigerator, she opened it and poured herself a glass of milk with ice. She could drink that all day every day. She tried to drink coffee, but hadn't acquired a taste for it yet. Drinking milk helped to calm her when she was nervous and alone.

Too wired up to go back to sleep, Milya pulled out a chair and sat down at the kitchen table looking about the room.

The white tiled floor had little specks of black sprinkled through it. There was a unique shine to it.

Inhaling and blowing out a deep breath, wishing to herself, "If only I could return Home." What made her do this for Zaria?

For some time now, that question had been taunting her mind.

Zaria Monroe was an old and dear friend of Milya's. They had known each other before high school and had been best friends since that time.

It was a strange request on Zaria's part to ask her to do this big favor, but hey, what are best friends for. At the time, Milya didn't think about it, she just leaped at an opportunity to put everything behind her for a while, especially Rick.

It seemed strange now that she had not heard from her friend. Zaria claimed that she could not teach her class this summer because something had come up. Pondering that thought, Milya had no idea what that something could be, though it was unlike her friend not to go into detail about it.

Milya was taking leave from both of her jobs in New York City to decide what career move she wanted to make. She had experience as a Broker, and she taught school at night.

She liked the excitement and different possibilities brokerage could bring, but found fulfillment in teaching young adults.

She gave her students a challenge, made them think for themselves, and gave them the opportunity to come up with alternative solutions.

So why was it now beginning to be a problem for her? Why had she not made up her mind? Milya knew the answer, but thought it was best not to think about the man she was fighting so hard not to love.

Reminiscing about their first encounter, Milya had to laugh to herself. They met at a dinner party a year or so ago and kept in touch. They had talked to each other quite a bit over the phone discussing practical investments. One day, out of the blue, Rick asked her to have dinner with him.

She always declined his appealing offers.

For about three weeks, after that invitation, they could not catch up with one another. Messages were left with both parties answering services.

It was about mid-week when she decided to go to the library and do a little research on a project she was about to give her class. She always liked to know more than they did on any given assignment. Walking up to the building, Milya was entering the revolving doors when something caught her eye. She knew that it had to have been him, because only one man could look like that.

He was casually dressed. He wore a black button down collarless shirt, black designer belt with a pair of khaki pants, black socks with khaki strips and black Florsheim shoes. He could not see the pleasurable look she had in her eyes. She really would love to feel his body next to hers. Little did she know then that her most fondish wish would be granted later that day.

One look at him and it was obvious that he worked out. His biceps flexed every time he moved his arms to write. He was standing at the receptionist desk. Milya thought "I bet he's trying to come on to her." But then he turned and noticed her standing in the door way.

Milya walked past him to turn down the first isle she came upon. He simply followed. Standing directly behind her, Rick whispered lightly, "Ms. Hargrove, it is good to see you in person again. Now that you are within my reach, I will simply not take no for an answer."

Turning to face him, her reply was, "I don't think that a question has been asked that would require an answer."

"You are so right, " he stated. "Will you have dinner with me tonight? If not tonight, have lunch with me now."

She really did not trust herself around him. His eyes were hazel brown and long eye lashes framed those eyes. His mustache looked like it had just been trimmed, and my God, he had naturally wavy hair. He was so smooth and very sure of himself.

Becoming aware that she had not answered his question, Milya said, "I think it's time we have that dinner you've been suggesting."

"Good, I am a wonderful cook Milya, and I would like the opportunity to impress you with a little of my culinary skills. Let's say I pick you up around five thirty this evening."

Thinking to herself, "Now he doesn't know where I live, so how can he come and pick me up"...Yes this was a slick one.

"If you would give me your address, I'll be there on time I promise," was Milya's reply.

He immediately wrote the address down on a piece of paper, folded it, and placed it in her hand, rubbing her fingers with his hand before returning them to his side.

Goose bumps trickled all over her body.

She had to refrain from shivering outwardly.

"I'll see you tonight then," was all that he said before he turned and left her standing in the isle alone.

Watching him leave, she had good visual access to his body. He had long muscular legs that made her breath quicken at the thought of what he could do with them. His buns were nice and firm, and from what she saw, he could really be something to work with. "Oh"...she thought, "tonight may be a glorious night."

Waiting to make sure that he had left, she strolled out of the doors, got into her car and headed for home. The school project was forgotten. What could she wear that would make his mouth water was her last thought before she focused on the drive home.

Pulling into the condo's parking garage, she barely had the car in park before she jumped out and hurried to the door. She had just come up with the perfect outfit. Milya was about five feet seven inches, and her skin was a beautiful cinnamon brown. She had a short stylish haircut that had that fade affect in the back. Her hair was a brownish black which always had body and a gloss to it. Her eyes were oval shaped and her eyebrows were perfectly arched. She was a very attractive woman.

Ignoring everything in the house, she went straight to her bedroom closet and pulled out her shimmering grape colored, silk crepe, A-line, flare tail dress with the matching jacket. The dress was low cut and showed just the right amount of cleavage with a zipper up the back. The jacket came down to her hips which would put all the attention she needed on the lower part of her body.

Pearl ear-rings and the matching necklace would grace her features as well. Adding the finishing touch, she would wear her laced garter belt, panties and bra, and her pearl colored stockings with the two and one half inch Nine West pearl pumps.

On the drive to his house, she wondered many things, how he would perceive her, would they have a great time, could he cook and what would it be like to have him as her man?????

Sighing, she hoped for the best. Pushing the button as she pulled up to the entrance, Milya's pulse quickened.

There was an answer in a voice that was so familiar to her, "come on up." That's exactly what she did.

When she reached the door to where he lived, it was open and he was standing there watching her approach.

"Good evening," Rick said.

She smiled, returning her own greeting, "Hello, how are you?"

"Please do come in." Standing aside, he extended his arms gesturing for her to come inside. He had Paul Taylor's jazz playing softly in the background, and the lights had been dimmed. Taking her handbag and placing it on the table just inside of the door, he asked, "would you like to dance Ms. Hargrove?"

Breathlessly she answered "yes."

Following him, she approached a room in which one wall was made of glass. Decorative blinds adorned that wall and were barely open, just enough to view the city below. The condominiums in which he lived were highrisers.

Staring in a weat the Milya was not prepared, suddenly twirled around and against a rock solid body. Lovely sight, for she was pressed hard.

Falling into step, moving her body to the music with his, instantly she noticed three things. First of all, he could hold her in a way that made her want to melt.

Secondly, It felt good to be held by him, and the third thing was that he was a wonderful dancer.

Placing a hand on his shoulder, she glanced up at him and looked into his eyes as they rocked to the music together.

Drawing her close, he could smell her fragrance, which reminded him of an ocean breeze. Guiding her head to his chest, he placed both hands around her waist, loosing himself in the magic of the moment.

She was so close to him that she could hear his heart beat. At that second, she wanted to get even closer. Feeling the warmth oozing from his body to hers, she also felt something nudge her near her waist.

She thought, "surely it's not what I think it is, and definitely not as large as it feels." Stepping back quickly, Milya asked, "Is dinner ready yet?"

Caught completely off guard, Rick opened his eyes and mumbled, "pardon me, dinner will be served in five minutes." Stalking away, walking pompously, he turned and went toward the kitchen.

With all of her might, Milya tried to relax, but curiosity was killing her. She wanted to look at that part of his body that extended with power. Excitement building like exploding firecrackers, Milya knew she would just simply have to ask him if she could look at what must be his most prized possession.

Returning to the room, Rick said, "please follow me." Trailing behind him, she could be envision Rick making love to her.

As she entered the kitchen, the spread she saw laid before her was magnificent. A delightful mixture of fresh fruit and juices were neatly arranged inside a cantaloupe. Crusty Italian garlic bread sticks were laid atop a checkered napkin and placed inside a basket. The steak kebabs, which looked very enticing, were honey glazed sirloins and crisp vegetables skewered and broiled.

Medium stem wine glasses were half filled with white wine. At first sight, her mouth drooled, and she wanted to taste everything.

One would have to have seen it to believe it. Voicing her thoughts aloud, "You didn't really prepare this yourself did you?"

"Why of course I did," he replied. "I come from a long line of excellent cooks and besides, being a bachelor, one must know how to cook in order to survive."

Smiling, he pulled a chair out to seat Milya so they could start enjoying their meal.

After a few sips of wine, Milya more relaxed. She realized that she feel comfortable around Rick. felt could The conversation flowed and time slipped by. Glancing down at her watch, she noticed that it was nine thirty p.m. Facing him she said, "I really must leave, the hour has grown late."

Rick made a facial expression implying that she had truly hurt him with her words.

"Can you stay a little longer, I am enjoying your company very much?"

But her answer was still "no, I'm afraid I have a lot of work to do." She really did want to stay and investigate the source of her curiosity though.

Getting up from the table, they both walked toward the door. Retrieving her hand bag from the table, Milya turned to tell him that she had had a wonderful time, but he was leaning down when she turned, and his face was even with hers. She could not move. She couldn't even think. Their lips were only inches apart. Their breath brushing each other's face.

Holding her spellbound, Rick said, "thank you for sharing this lovely dinner with me Ms. Hargrove."

But before she could give a response, he was moving his lips against hers. His touch was soft but firm. A moan escaped her lips, and he deepened the kiss. She leaned into him letting him support her weight, and for a moment she thought that she was lost in heaven.

He was lifting her towards the direction they had just come in his arms turning she noticed the direction and by sheer force Milya pulled back. "No Rick", in a weak voice, "I don't think we should do this."

"We don't have to do anything you don't want to do Milya, but please just let me kiss you once more before you leave."

Not waiting for her consent, the magic he could do so well with his lips started all over again. Grabbing him around his neck, Milya held on for dear life, holding on to him as if he was her life line.

How long they had been lying atop his bed, she did not know. All she could concentrate on was the here and now, the way he was caressing her body and kissing heated paths along her neck.

What had become of her jacket, and how her dress became unzipped to reveal her lace bra was puzzling? But what he was making her feel took precedence over everything else.

Her stomach clenched as he rubbed her nipples with his hand while he kissed her. Milya thought that she might die of pleasure at the pressure he was applying, when his mouth replaced his hands.

Feeling his manhood extend with the excitement, Milya stopped all movement. Rick asked, "What's wrong?"

"What is this?" was her reply.

"What are you talking about?" Rick asked.

Milya then slid her hand down the length of his manhood.

"My God, is all of that you?" "Yes" he said.

"Turn on the lamp" was all that Milya said.

Rick could not believe her, but he did as she asked. Milya knew that her request was a strange one, but she had to know what she was dealing with. Although she was tipsy, she knew what she felt, and it felt extra, extra-large.

Rick's pants were already unzipped, and he had on a pair of silk boxers. She pulled the top of his underwear down, so that she could see for herself what it was that he had in his possession, and his manhood tumbled out. Immediately she had to start taking deep breaths.

Milya didn't know that any human being could be so large. If you balled both of your fists up and placed them together knuckles side by side, in front of each other, that would give you an idea of how large his crest was.

After making the big discovery, Milya looked up at Rick with shock written across her face and said, "I don't think we should do this after all." Gathering her clothes, Milya made a hasty exit.

"How could he have cheated on me?" Pushing those thoughts aside, noticing that she was still at the kitchen table, Milya made her way back to her bedroom, wondering how long she had been sitting there staring at the speckled floor.

Zaria left her apartment for Milya's use, actually it was more on the style of a duplex. It was a two bed and bathroom apartment with a kitchen, den and living room.

The rooms were large, nothing like you would find in the city. The den had hardwood floors that glistened like crystal. Who kept them that way, she didn't know, but decided that she would use the same product her mother used when cleaning their floors at home.

All of the rooms were painted antique white, except for the bathrooms. They had border trimmings and were painted with a multi-colored paint. They looked as if someone had taken a sponge and placed it on the wall several times. The pink, green, purple and yellow colors were truly beautiful. Decorating the bathrooms had to have been easy due to the many colors you could choose from.

After making her bed, Milya went to her closet and chose her attire for the day.

Being in Mississippi during the summer could be a long and trying experience. The mosquitos could be harmful. Just yesterday a mosquito bit her and she hit it, but the thing just kept biting her. With a little more force in her swing, she was able to rid herself of the insect. One thing is for sure about the Delta, you must be prepared in the summer.

A multi-colored t-strap sundress, that could be tied just as a wraparound skirt, with a split in the back was selected. To complete her Sunday's attire, Milya chose her black two and one-half-inch sandals and a black straw sun hat.

She wanted to look presentable when she went to visit Zaria's mom. Zaria had a lot of relatives that all lived nearby, and when a strange vehicle drove down their street, nearly all of them came out to see who it was. They didn't mind talking about you-to-your face either.

Milya wanted to ask Miss Sadie, Zaria's mother, a few questions. Checking her reflection in the oblong mirror in her bedroom, Milya walked around the apartment securing windows and making sure lights were off. She left the bathroom nightlights on as well as the light above the stove, because she didn't know how long she would be gone.

Thinking to herself, "If the grocery list could be found, that I made last night, I could be on my way. Oh forget it, I'll find it when I return."

Satisfied with her usual inspection, Milya picked up her keys and purse and walked out of the apartment. From the heat that assaulted her the minute she opened the door, Milya thought "today is going to be a scorcher." She was glad to get an early start. She walked to her two-toned black and grey Lexus. It was a five speed with grey leather interior, FM. AM stereo, CD player and an electric sun-roof. The brown glossy panel inside near the dashboard gave it that certain flair. She really liked the sleek look of this car.

CHAPTER TWO

Across the street, parked about two houses down, Milya's apartment was being watched. Lying back in a somewhat reclining position, sweating from the heat, the person's mind was beginning to wonder if she would ever leave her home.

It had been a long night and day since instructions had been given to watch the house and all who lived within it. They were to take notes of any comings and goings and if deemed necessary trail, but to do it discreetly. When the time came, they would be given permission to do what needed to be done, but not until then...."

Milya opened the car and slipped gracefully behind the wheel. Placing her foot on the clutch, she put the keys in the ignition and started the car.

The silent hum of the engine was like music to her ears. After finding the reverse gear, Milya backed the car out of the designated parking space and headed towards the highway.

Listening to her favorite radio station 66.2, the oldies but goodies station, Milya started to sing along with Natalie Cole's "Our Love."

Milya noticed the scenery. She had always loved the Delta for its flat land. Hardly ever would one have to worry about driving a stick shift car and rolling backwards on top of a hill when people are entirely too close behind you.

Looking out of the window as she drove, she noticed that the grass was a comely green hue and the fields had been recently cut. This city had truly grown since she left nine years ago.

Businesses were up everywhere. Along the highway, restaurants, hotels, car-lots and gas stations, in addition to other operations, filled up both sides of the avenue.

Before she knew it, Milya had reached her turn. Easing out of the traffic and off the highway, Milya headed toward Miss Sadie's house.

How does one inquire without causing alarm? Trying to come up with a plan, Milya was considering asking Zaria's mother questions without producing any suspicion just in case something had happened to her friend.

After watching the car pull out with only one occupant, the unknown observer that was seen earlier in the morning before dawn, felt that a tail on the driver of the car was not needed at this time. Instead, a thorough search of the apartment should be done.

The individual left the car and walked up to the back door instead of the person. With the sun beaming in through the half-open mini blinds, lights were not needed. The streets could be seen from inside the apartment's partially closed blinds.

The search began with opening up and looking inside of every drawer and cabinet, room by room. While sifting through papers, mail and magazines, the person thought, "" it has to be here."" The search must continue until it is found or someone will have to deal with the consequences.

Walking past what must have been her bedroom, the observer stopped to admire the astonishing decor of the room.

Images were framed with mats that added livelihood to each picture. Along one wall of the room, an antique brass bed sat next to a window.

The comforter set had matching sheets. It appeared to be a Miramar design. The night stand with a lamp and digital clock stood next to the bed.

The carpet was a plush hunter green, soft to each step made. An armoire with feminine products atop it lined another side of the room as well as a matching dressing table. There was also a leather rocker/recliner with pockets on the sides. This room was full of warmth.

Wanting to start the search in this room next, the person looked into the pockets of the chair on both sides. Coming up empty handed, the search then shifted to every drawer in that room and in the entire house.

Turning down Madeline Lane, Milya noticed that Miss Sadie was just coming out of her house. She looked as if she was just about to leave.

Milya pulled up behind Miss Sadie's car and got out. "Hello," Milya said, "Does Miss Sadie Monroe live here?," knowing all along who she was talking to.

"Milya Hargrove, is that you?"

"Yes rna' am."

"Well then, you know very well who I am."

"Yes I do," Milya said and you're looking so like a teenager, that's why I hardly even recognized you." Miss Sadie laughed, "girl, you still know how to tell a good lie don't you."

"No rna' am," was Milya's response as she walked towards Miss Sadie and gave her a hardy hug.

"Well honey, I was about to leave and get out on it, but since you're in town, I can spare you a few minutes. Come on in. Are you hungry? Would you like something to drink?"

"No thank you," Milya said.

"Zaria told me that you might be coming home soon and that she hoped it wasn't when she had to leave to do some research for the college" Miss Sadie was saying.

Milya's mind started trying to recall whether Zaria had mentioned that to her.

Blocking out Miss Sadie's voice, Milya knew for a fact that Zaria had not said a word about it. If research for the college was truly necessary, why would she volunteer to teach a summer school session?

Knowing that something must be wrong, she focused her attention back on Miss Sadie's voice.

"Milya! Did you hear anything I just said?"

"Yes ma'am."

"No you didn't", Mrs. Sadie said cutting her reply off. "I said it is good to see you again and that Zaria had really hoped that you would get a chance to come home, but not when she was working."

Now, Milya knew that something was wrong. She would have to find out exactly what it was on her own. Smiling at Mrs. Sadie, she said, "Where is everyone? I've never come to visit you in the past and had you entirely to myself."

"Honey, we spotted your car a mile away, and I told everyone to stay put until I had a chance to talk with you myself. You see, Zaria had already described your car to me, therefore I knew who you were, and besides she said that you would be coming home soon, so I've been kind of looking for you."

"Is that right," Milya said. "what else has Zaria told you?"

"She said that you have a nice looking man in your life, so where is he?"

"Zaria talks too much, and anyway, we are apart right now."

"What's the problem?" Miss Sadie asked.

"I don't really want to go into it right now, but I will be here a little while and I might get around to telling you about it."

"All I have to say is that men will be men, and you are not the first woman who is going through whatever it is you're going through and you won't be the last. As long as he respects you and your house and he's a good man, you can probably deal with the rest. Now that's all I have to say."

Milya looked at Miss Sadie and said, " you always did shoot straight from the hip didn't you."

"Baby, there is no other way to shoot."

Both ladies started laughing.

Standing up, Miss Sadie said," Child as you saw, I was on my way out when you pulled up."

"So what are you saying Miss Sadie?"

Milya asked.

"I'm saying that you've got to go because I'm about to leave here. We can chat another time. I have a hair appointment this morning."

"You look spiffy to me."

"You are so right. I'm just going to touch up the rough edges a little bit. You know, I like looking new and not used."

At that statement both ladies laughed as they made their way out the door to find three ladies were waiting for them.

"Hey Milya, How are you, and what brought you back to the big city?"

Forcing her smile to stay in place, Milya spoke to all three of Miss Sadie's messy sisters.

Aunt Aria, Aunt Detra and Aunt Jo were all asking her a thousand questions at once. "Is this your car or did you rent it? What do you really do now for a living? Have you found yourself a man yet?"

Milya cut them off by saying, "Since neither of you have seen me in quite a while, the least you could do is give me a hug, and to answer your questions, It's none of your business" ,looking sharply at the three ladies. Milya said her good-byes and kissed Miss Sadie on her cheek before she walked to her car.

Milya backed up and pulled out of the drive way. Blowing her horn, she waved goodbye, thinking to herself, "boy did I just miss a horrible interrogation."

After searching the house room by room and coming up empty handed, the person returned to the bedroom once more, hoping that the item in question would somehow appear.

The person lifted the comforter, searched under the mattress and moved pillows around. The intruder let out a heavy sigh. Thinking aloud, the person said, "I hope this Ms Hargrove has nothing to do with this because she's a very pretty woman, and I would hate to have to kill her."

Just as those words were spoken, the person spotted her car returning to its original parking space.

Rushing to put everything back in order in the room, keys were heard unlocking a door. Being caught in situations similar to this all of the time, waiting the victim out would not be a problem. Stepping into a corner in the den, down the hall from her bedroom, seemed to be a good place to wait her out.

Milya entered the kitchen and turned on the lights. She left the back door open, and walked down the hall to her bedroom, to get the money she had placed in her drawer. She needed to retrieve her grocery list she had written earlier.

Speaking out loud to herself she said, "today I think I will run by the grocery store and Wal-Mart for additional household supplies."

She opened the drawer in her bedroom and got the extra money she needed. As Milya turned to leave, she noticed that her comforter was lifted on one side. It looked as if someone had pulled the comforter back to look under the bed.

"Hmm... I thought I made my bed before I left. Maybe I was looking for something and left it like that. Oh well, I guess I did." she said aloud. She smoothed out the covers on the bed, and turned to look at herself in the mirror before heading back out. She walked back down the hall and she stopped at the den's door.

Not wanting to breathe hard for fear of being discovered, the person barely moved. The lady's voice and footsteps could be heard. Every move she made was noticed.

Looking into the den, she thought, "I should open the blinds and let a little more light into this room."

Hearing her stop at the door of the den, the person hunched down behind a chair in the far corner of the room. Milya thought she heard a sound. Looking around the room, she did not notice anything unusual.

She walked to the window and opened the blinds fully to let the sunlight shine through. As she turned to leave, she saw the grocery list she had written the night before laying on the chair in the far corner of the den.

She bent over to retrieve the grocery list and the air from the movement she made, caused the list to fall onto the floor. Picking up the note, she paused to look at what she thought was the back of an earring lying on the floor, before turning to leave the room. As she left, she made sure that she locked the back door and returned to her car.

A sigh of relief was felt from the person who was hiding in the den. The intruder said, "that is what you truly say is a close call." Standing up from the hunched position, the intruder looked around. All precautions were made to be certain that the lady had left before an exit of the apartment could be made.

Walking back to the parked car, a phone call was placed to the authorities about the search of the apartment and questions asked about what steps should be taken next.

With the household shopping behind her, Milya made her way back home, put up all of her purchases and changed clothes for a relaxing evening at home.

Now was the time to try and somehow contact Zaria. Maybe she should call her friends Steven and Katie McDougal. They have always been there for her when she needed them the most.

Picking up the telephone, Milya dialed the McDougals. While she was waiting for the other line to start ringing, which never did, she heard her name being whispered. Apparently someone had called her before she started to dial, therefore her phone did not ring.

"Milya!" "Milya!" "Stop dialing and listen to me." "Zaria is that you? Girl where are you?" Milya asked.

"Shut up and listen, we're in trouble!"

"Who's in trouble?," Milya asked, but Zaria kept right on talking.

"We need your help. We need you to," was all that Milya heard because the line had gone dead.

"Zaria!" "Zaria!" Milya kept calling, but didn't get a response. Not knowing what to do or even what to think about the call she had just received, Milya stared at the phone she held in her hand. She hung up and started dialing again.

As Milya nervously dialed the McDougals, she knew that this was not the time to lose her head.

The phone was answered on the second ring. "Hi Steven this is Milya. I need to talk to you and Katie."

"Hold on one minute," Steven yelled, "Katie, pick up the other phone."

"Yeah," Katie said.

"Hi Katie, this is Milya."

"Hey girl, what's up?"

"Well, I think that we have a problem."

"Oh-Oh, what's up" Katie replied rather than asked.

"I think Zaria's in trouble, what kind I don' t know."

Milya started talking really fast. "I haven't heard from Zaria since I've been here and it's unlike her not to have called by now. Tonight, just before I called you, she called me talking extremely low. She said, we are in trouble. I asked her who's in trouble, and she said we need you to-and then the phone went dead."

Katie was the first to respond. "Steven, I told you that something was fishy."

"I know what you said, first of all, we need to remain calm and do some serious brain storming."

"Milya are you all right?" Steven asked. "Yeah, it's just scary. If I didn't know Zaria, I would write this off as a big joke, but hell, I know she wouldn't play a joke like this on me."

"Milya why is it that every time you get into trouble, it's always what are we going to do?," Katie asked.

"Now the two of you know that I Love you so much, I would never dream of leaving you out on any of my little projects."

Steven, Katie and Milya met while they were in college. They also became good friends. Steven and Katie married shortly after graduating and now have a seven-year old daughter and a three year old son.

The McDougals were familiar with Zaria through Milya. They

all got together once and a while.

Katie asked, "are you afraid to stay in the apartment alone, or do you need to come here and stay with us?"

"No, no, I'm not afraid. I have my baseball bat you know." "I don't know kungfu, but I'll beat the shit out of somebody, and besides, I can bite, scratch, kick and holler. The two of you would definitely hear me."

Everyone laughed. "Milya, I'm going to check into some things and I will give you a call back," Steven said, "but if you hear from her again, don't hesitate to call us."

Steven said good-bye and hung up. He knew that the girls would want to talk a little longer, and he would give Rick Cantello a call to let him know that Milya was going to need his help.

"Katie, is the line clear?"

"Yes girl, go ahead and say it."

"Katie, I miss him so much, but he'll never know it."

"Why not?"

"Do we really have to go through that again? You know why I had to leave and break-off the engagement. How would you feel If your man had another woman pregnant?"

"Wait Milya, you don't know if it is his."

"That's true, but the bottom line is that he's been there and he shouldn't have been. If you are going to go there, the least you could do is activate your bullet proof shield."

"OK, you do have a point, but we also know that there are some trifling women out there who want a hard working man."

"I don't care, right now I'm just not ready to forgive him even if he is all under my skin. I can't even wash him off girl."

"Hal ... yes you can, hell you just need to change your brand of soap. That shit you've been using probably doesn't even work anymore."

Laughing, Milya said, "I knew that I could count on you to keep me stable. Now that I am sane, what do you think about Zaria?"

"I am willing to bet you that she got mixed up in some of her brother's mess again, Katie said."

"You know what, you are probably right, and if that's true, I should be scared. That boy."

"What do you mean boy, hell, he's twenty-five years old, Katie interjected."

"Well that "want-to-be" man is never going to get his life together. He's too damn crooked and he's a bum. Always acting as if he's got it going on. I think that he's into drugs myself but don't quote me because I'm not certain."

"Milya, we all know that man is a no good...., I can't even come up with a word for him."

"Well, all I know is if he's gotten Zaria into something that is life threatening, I'm going to kick his you know what."

"Milya, are you going to kick his ass?"....

"Yes I am. Girl let me go, remember y'all are in my pocketbook." "Why is it that everytime you call us, we are in your pocketbook, but when we call you, you can talk all day and night?" "Because it's two of y'all, and only one of me. Now with that being said, good bye," Milya hung up the phone in Katie's face.

Sitting up in her bed watching TV, Milya decided that she didn't want to stay in the apartment alone. Gathering her over-night bag, she put enough clothes in it to last her two to three days. She figured that she might as well go and visit her mom. It would only be an hours' drive depending upon the traffic. After locking the house, Milya got into her car and headed home. Adjusting her rear-view mirror, Milya thought, "I must be paranoid, I'm looking at every car that passes by as if I'm being tailed. I don't know what it is, but something doesn't feel right."

Milya pulled into the garage of her mother's home, reached for her things and got out of the car. Just knowing that she was at her mom's made her feel so much better.

CHAPTER THREE

Milya and her mother were very close. It wasn't anything she couldn't tell her mom, that is, if she wanted to. Tonight she hoped her mother was in a talking mood because she had a lot of things she wanted to say.

Reba Hargrove was a single parent who somehow always knew when her child was troubled. She was expecting to see Milya soon due to the fact that her fiancé had called and said that he was on his way to do some type of investigation and had asked her if he could stay with their Uncle Bennie.

"Rick, this is Steven McDougal, give me a call as soon as you get this message, it's"....Cutting into the conversation, Rick said, "Hey man, what's up?" "I guess you're screening your calls huh." "No, actually I'm just getting in."

How's Katie and the kids? I haven't heard from you in over a month." "Rick, I'm going to cut to the chase. Milya needs you. We think that Zaria is in some kind of trouble." Steven went on to explain what Milya told him and Katie.

"Milya may be dragged into something that she knows nothing about. Besides, I believe that Zaria's brother, Stan, is into some heavy shit. I didn't mention that to the girls earlier because I didn't want to upset them," Steven said. "I've seen Stan with known mobsters. Even though he appears to be a bum, he's actually an intelligent man. He is good with computers and wires-kind of a handy-man like yourself."

"Yeah right" Rick said. "He couldn't be that damn handy, but Milya's welfare is my number one concern. I fucked up and I admitted that to her, but it wasn't like she thinks. We will have time to talk about that later, right now, I'm going to call in a few favors and see If I can find out what's going on."

Rick continued, "You know, in my line of work, you meet all kinds of crooked motherfuckers. Once I start the background check, I'm taking the first flight I can get to the Delta. I think I will stay with Milya' s Uncle Bennie and lay low. I don't want Milya to know that I'm there right away. I'll straighten things out with her later."

"My friend, that will be some hard shit to do" Steven replied.

"Yeah, I know. First I have to call Milya's mother and inform her of some things, then I'll make that trip. By the way, where exactly is Milya staying? Out of all the times you've called me and we've talked, you've never told me exactly where she is."

"Buddy you've got to do a little work on your own. You did say that you were good at finding out what you wanted, and if I am correct, Milya is what you want, isn't she? Besides, Milya, Katie and I are very good friends, I can't betray her, not even for you."

"Yes, Steven, you know that she's all I ever wanted."

"Well then my friend, I suggest you let the begging begin, you old hound dog you."

"Fuck you Steven."

"Fuck you! see you later."

At the end of the street, another phone call was made to the authorities. "The lady traveled to her mother' s house. I trailed her from a safe distance. You were right, she brought along a little suitcase. Do you still have the two of them? OK, I'll be in to interrogate them. Answers will be given."

Using her key to enter her mother's house, Milya pushed opened the side door. She did not want to wake up her mother, so she tipped across the kitchen floor, bumping her toe as she went along.

"Shit! that hurt." "What did you say?"

Surprised by her mother's voice, Milya asked, "Mom, what are you doing up?"

"I'm waiting for you."

"How did you know that I was coming?"

"I told you that I have, what is called, a mother's intuition. Back to the cursing."

Holding up her hand, Milya said, "Mom, I apologize. You were not supposed to hear that, but now, I have always told you that my mouth is bad. If you should ever walk upon me and I don't see you, just keep on walking. If any of your friends should come and tell you that they heard me cursing, don't argue with them because I probably was. By the way, I'm trying to stop. Isn't that great?"

Reba just shook her head. "So Milya, what's going on?"

"I don't really know, but I do know this, Zaria is in some serious trouble. If it is because of her brother, there is no telling what it could be."

"You know, that boy is crazy. Do you feel comfortable staying in Zaria's house?"

"Yeah, I don't have a problem with it." "Did you ever consider that someone could be watching her house." "Oh mama, don't say that." "Why not?"

"Because you'll make me scared."

"Well I tell you what, we'll both drink us some milk with ice and try to get some sleep, and we will figure things out in the morning."

"Who is it?"

"It's me Uncle Bennie, open up."

"Me who? Reveal yourself. Don't fuck with me this time of night 'cause I'll cut the funk from your ass."

Bennie was Milya's great-uncle. He was seventy-five years old and very handy with a knife.

"Bennie, this is Rick Cantello. Didn't Mrs. Hargrove tell you that I was coming."

"Yep, she sho' did, but you must think that I'm a damn fool to open my door up to anybody who say this me. These folks are crazy now-a-days."

Bennie opened the door and let Rick in. "Uncle Bennie, can we talk low and move about quietly?"

"What the fuck for?"

"Milya is next door at her mom's."

"Huh..so what you want me to do is to be quiet in my own house cause you can't hold on to your dick. I ain't told you to go slipping and sliding with that gal and get a baby. So I ain't gonna walk light in my own house for you."

"She cut your ass loose, didn't she?" "I know she did, I know my nephew" (Bennie called all of his nieces his nephews and vice versa) Rick couldn't do anything but shake his head and laugh. "OK Uncle Bennie, just tell me where you will let me sleep for the next couple of nights?"

"Who said you could stay?" "Well I thought."

"I know what you thought, you thought Milya wouldn't leave you but she did. I ought to make you sleep outside like a dog. Go on in the other bed room in there."

"Thank you so much Uncle Bennie." "I ain't your damn uncle."

"Stan, I can't see, where are we?"

"Zaria, just stay calm and let me do all of the talking."

"What do you mean stay calm. I was on my way to meet my brother and was kidnapped at gun point. I couldn't even tell what or who the person was, and you want me to remain calm. If I could see you, I would kill you, she yelled."

"This is such a wonderful scene to hear and see a sister and brother speak so lovely to one another, a voice interjected strangely." The sound of the voice was strange and muffled. You couldn't tell if it was a man or woman talking.

Footsteps could be heard all around Zaria. Suddenly she felt excruciating pain. Whoever the voice belonged to was squeezing her arm hard.

"Ouch", Zaria yelled. "That hurt!"

The voice said, "Give us what we want and no harm will come to you."

"What do you want?" Zaria asked.

"Leave her alone," Stan said.

Bump, was the only sound that Zaria heard.

"Oh GOD! please don't harm my brother. Stan please give them what they want." (not being able to see, she didn't know that Stan was unconscious, lying on the floor.)

"He didn't hear you lady"; the voice said, "He's been knocked out." Zaria tensed at those words and didn't move another muscle.

"When and if he wakes up, you definitely won't be around. Take her away."

After settling down in his room, Rick could not keep his mind off of Milya, knowing that she was just a house away. He hadn't tasted her charms in a long time.

Getting up, he pulled on an old pair of blue jeans and a V-neck t-shirt. He had to get out and get some fresh air. Leaving his room, he left the door ajar, not wanting to make any noise.

Uncle Bennie just happened to be passing by. "Boy, where are you going? I hope it's not to see my nephew this time of night."

"No it isn't old man. Would you mind your own business."

"I got your old man," Uncle Bennie said. Laughing, Rick left the house and stood outside on the garret, as uncle Bennie called it, for a minute. His eyes had to adjust to the darkness of night. Glancing around, Rick tried to notice if anything looked suspicious.

He didn't think so, but there was a steady stream of cars passing by on the adjacent street. He was expecting a call before morning from some friends about Zaria's brother. Closing his eyes, he could smell Milya-no-he could taste her, her lips, her breast, her skin.

Dreaming of wild love making, Milya could actually feel Rick and the things he could do to her. In her mind, she was actually thinking of how good it was to have him back in her life.

Milya woke up to look around the room through half closed eyes; she knew that she was in the room all alone. So why were her vibes for him so strong? That question plagued her. Feeling hot, she laid on top of the sheets. Not able to hold her eyes open any longer, Milya drifted back off to sleep.

Though it seemed like he was fighting a losing battle, Rick finally made his way to Milya' s bedroom window. Since he had been to their house many times in the past, he knew exactly where her room was. Peering through the window, he couldn't see anything. With a little push, the window started to rise. Rick thought, "this is something teenagers do."

Someone had apparently oiled the window seal because it didn't make a sound as it was being raised, and he was very grateful for that Rick attempted to ease through the window.

Trying to be careful, Rick stuck something in his hand. "Ouch!" "What the fuck is that?" He said softly to himself. "Be quite and calm," he reminded himself. "You just climbed through your girl's window."

He was holding his hand as he turned, and what he saw stole his breath away. There she was lying on top of the covers in a satin cream nightie. It had t-straps and she wasn't wearing underwear. The way she slept caused her gown to reveal one side of her left hip. She was lying on her stomach with her left leg extended outward. She was in a great position to be kissed all over.

He tipped towards her making his way to her bedside. Placing his hands on the mattress gently, he bent down on his knees. For a moment, he just looked and admired her body.

When his manhood stiffened, he knew then and there that he had to have her. Kissing her buttocks softly, he embraced them lightly with his hands.

Milya's dream made her feel so good that she never wanted to awaken again. Ironically, she was dreaming along the same line as his performance. Just having him touch her again in her dream, making her weak all over, made her sigh in her sleep.

The sound that she made was like music to Rick's ears. He needed no further encouragement, especially when she moved and gave him easier access to her anatomy.

Easing her legs slightly apart, he found her clitoris with his fingers. He could feel her becoming moist for him. Sliding his finger towards the center of her womanhood, he almost exploded himself. He could hear her intake breaths of air.

He thought back to times in the past when he used to awaken her like this. How could he have been such a fool to make the mistake he made.

Getting control of himself, he was about to replace his hands with his lips when he heard Milya's name being called. He could hear footsteps coming down the hall.

He jumped to his feet and retraced his steps, Rick was glad that he left the window open because the dive he had to make could have been a world's record.

"Milya!" "Milya!" "Wake up!" Reba said.

Milya jumped at the sound of her mother's voice and the shaking of her arm, "What is it mom? Is there something wrong?"

"Honey that's what I want to know."

"Are you ill?"

"No, why?"

"Because you were in here moaning like a sick puppy."

Remembering her dream, Milya reached for the sheets and pulled them up over her body.

Reba said," I don't know why you're trying to hide your naked ass from me, you know I helped to conceived therefore I know what you look like."

Milya was wondering if her mother could see her blush.

"Was I that loud mom?"

"Yes, why do you think I came in here shaking you like I did. You really sounded as if you were in pain. What were you dreaming about that had you so tied up in knots?"

Milya asked GOD for his forgiveness before she told her mother this lie, "actually I don't know. Now you're going to have me up for the rest of the night trying to remember what it was."

"Girl if I know you, you will be asleep before I leave this room. Good-night for the second time."

Milya responded, "good-night."

Feeling as if she was wringing wet with sweat, Milya thought, nothing could feel as real as the dream she had just experienced. She noticed that she was damp. "Oh my, I must get this man out of my system." Milya went to the bathroom to freshen herself up before going back to bed.

Outside sitting on Uncle Bennie's steps, Rick had to be patient and wait for his nerves to calm down. What he had done was truly risky, and he could have blown everything.

CHAPTER FOUR

Milya awoke to the smell of bacon in the house. She knew that her mother was cooking breakfast. Milya still could not get over the dream she had last night.

Before joining her mother for breakfast, she decided to call Zaria's home and check the answering machine. Listening to the one message on the machine, Milya tried to figure out who Bethany was.

"Hi Zaria, this is Bethany, I'm looking for your brother. If you get this message, please have Stan call me. I'll be in town a few days and I would like to see you. Talk to you later, bye."

Milya thought, that had to have been Stan's last female companion. Zaria and Bethany didn't really see eye to eye, so why would she want to see Zaria? The answer to that puzzling question should be very interesting.

"Enough is enough, it's time to push those thoughts aside and enjoy the most important meal of the day," Milya said aloud to herself. She got out of bed, dressed and entered the kitchen.

"Good morning mother, how are you?"

"I'm doing great, what about you? It sounds like you had a rough night." "Actually, I slept rather well. I think that I am leaning toward giving Rick a call."

"Oh, are you now?"

"Yes. If we don't come up with something soon, I will have to rely on his expertise. He knows a lot of people and maybe one of them can help us find out what's going on."

"Yeah-right, any excuse will do."

"I assure you that that is the only reason I want to contact him."

"If you say so, but don't you think the police should be involved?"

"No mama, not yet. What could I tell them?"

"For starters you could say that your friend and her brother are missing."

"Honestly mama, I really don't know what to do." "Well I agree with you, Rick should be called. You never know, he might show up here within a moment's notice."

"You really like him, don't you?"

"I think he is a nice man, but I'm not the one who's got to like him, you do. Baby everybody has problems. For example, your teeth and your tongue fall out sometimes especially when you're chewing gum and one bites the other. You see, communication is the key Milya. When there's a barrier in your communication, all walls break down."

"I know mama."

"Now let's eat our food before it turns cold."

Zaria had been placed on what felt like an old mattress. She was blindfolded, but not gagged. Her hands were tied behind her back, not cutting into her flesh, but tight enough where she couldn't get out.

"GOD please help me. I'm scared and don't know what's going on, or where I am. Please protect me and be a fence all around me," Zaria prayed aloud.

The door opened as she ended her prayer, and the voice said, "here is a meal for you. This cup of water will cure your thirst. I'll be back to collect the dishes." Delta Heat Zaria felt her hands being released from their strong hold. "Which hand do you use the most, the voice asked?"

"My right hand." Her left hand was tied to something cold, perhaps steel. Placing an eating utensil, cup and plate in her hand, Zaria heard footsteps retreating and then a door closing.

She had been to scared to move, so she sat exactly where they left her. Listening intently, Zaria wanted to know if she still had company. "Is anyone there?" she asked, but didn't get a response. All she could hear was a swishing sound. That sound did nothing to help her realize where she was. Without her sight, she was hopelessly lost.

The aroma from the food made her stomach growl. She had been so caught up in everything that happened until she forgot she had not eaten.

Half scared to eat the food and half scared not to, Zaria moved her fingers over the plate. She picked up what felt like a chicken leg, and from the smell of it, she'd say it came from "Churches Chicken."

"Hello."

"Is Rick in?"

"Who you want?"

"Rick Cantello."

"Hold on, boy it's for you," Uncle Bennie said as he passed Rick the telephone.

"Rick Cantello speaking."

"Zaria was last seen being pushed into a rust colored Delta Eighty Eight with a Washington County license plate."

"I see. Is there any other information?"

"Yeah, that car is seen a lot at the docks, close to the casinos. We're still watching it. I'll call back if anything else comes up."

"Thanks, Rick said as he hung up the phone."

Uncle Bennie's telephone rang again. This time, Rick answered the phone.

"Hello."

"Rick this is Steven, did you get settled?"

"Yes, and it happened just like you thought it would."

"Was he that hard on you?"

"Yeah, Bennie throws hard verbal punches."

Both men laughed. "Steven, I have what's beginning to look like a lead. Some of my associates have been doing a little undercover work for me. She was seen in a rust colored Delta Eighty Eight that hangs out at the dock. I'm going down there to do a little snooping around tonight."

"Well I'm glad I caught you at a good time."

"Why, what's up."

"Does Milya know that you're there?"

"No, why?"

"She will after tonight."

"Why the hell would she know?"

"Katie and I will be in on the three o'clock flight. Milya has no idea that we're coming."

"What the fuck is going on?"

"Hold on and let me explain. Katie didn't think that it was a good idea for you to be so involved and risk your life without Milya knowing it."

"Your point being?"

"We're making it a team effort."

"You know that I work alone with only a few in my employ."

"Yes I do, but I couldn't talk Katie out of it. She's worried sick about Milya. The kids are already at her moms, and we are packed."

"I'm not picking your ass up, and I will not put Milya's life in danger. She is not to know."

"See you later," Steven said before he hung up the phone in Rick's face.

"Damn, that's fucked up," Rick replied. The conversation ended just as quickly as it began. Rick was mad, no he was steaming, almost as hot as fire. He wasn't exactly ready to face her. Rick knew this time would come, but he wanted to do it his way. "If I were a smoking man, I believe I could smoke an entire pack of cigarettes.

Feeling like he had to get a breath of fresh air, Rick said, "I must leave here."

After breakfast, Milya helped her mother with the household chores. Having cleaned almost every room vigorously, Milya still needed an outlet. She had a feeling that something was about to happen. Why couldn't she feel at ease? She was, after all, at home with her mother. Not able to stand being confined any longer, Milya decided to take a walk outside.

Milya's family's land was located near a wooded area. Behind their homes, a row of trees marked the beginning and the end of their property.

Rick stood just inside the first tier of trees. He saw Milya leaving her mother's house. Rick waited to see what course she would take before he made his move and made his presence known.

She strolled towards him. It was as if she could see him through the trees, Rick was thinking. He knew that he would stay where he was until she got right upon him before he approached her.

Sensing that someone was watching her, Milya walked slowly to the first row of trees. Rick called her name when she was five feet away from him.

Alarmed, Milya stopped dead in her tracks. She looked around trying to cover every inch of land. Then she spotted him. Not wasting one moment, she immediately ran in the other direction willing herself to lose him in the trees. This was her territory, and who knew it better than she did. As a child, she ran and played in this area for hours at a time.

"Dammit Milya!," Rick said before he took off after her. "Come back here!"

For every two steps she took, he only had to take one. He was upon her before she knew it. Avoiding his clutch, Milya dropped down to the ground and picked up a small sprig. She drew back and struck Rick on the arm with everything she had.

"Shit Milya!," Rick said. But before he could say another word, she hit him on his outer thigh.

Milya didn't wait to see what kind of damage she had done. She turned again and resumed running through the trees. How he caught her, she didn't know. Her breathing was so hard, until she drowned everything else out. She didn't hear him coming.

Rick cut her off with one smooth blow.

He made a dive, which caught her around the waist, and with

one tug, they fell to the ground.

Milya fell face down. Her entire body hurt. She thought her teeth were falling out of her mouth. Her neck felt as if it would snap. Not wanting to give in to a losing battle, Milya struggled wildly wanting to throw Rick off of her.

"Get away from me," Milya shouted. Opening her mouth made her teeth ache more.

Rick slid away from her body long enough to flip her over onto her back. His face was only inches from hers when Milya tried to slap him. Her hand was not half way to his face before he had it in his grasp.

Again Milya tried to get free, but all of her efforts were in vain. "If you don't stop moving your body in that bucking motion, I'm going to take you right here, right now," Rick said.

Milya froze immediately. She had not given any thought to what she was doing. All she wanted was to be free of his grasp.

Rick knew that he could not stop himself from becoming riged. The minute she started moving, his manhood began to throb. He wanted her in the worst way. Looking into her eyes, he could see tears gathering there.

Milya didn't want to cry. The water just somehow appeared in her eyes. Not only did she hurt from the fall, now she felt like she would explode from being captured. Though she wanted to despise him, her body reacted differently. It appeared to absorb the feel of him.

"Don't cry," Rick said as he kissed the corner of each of her eyes. He trailed kisses along her jawline down to the edge of her lips.

"Rick, stop it!" Milya said as she tried to kick him again. Moving his lips against hers, Rick said, "I'm going to kiss you." He knew that she would try to bite his lip or pull a similar stunt, but he was ready. Milya did try to bite him, but her plan backfired. The moment she opened her mouth, he entered hers forcefully, applying pressure to weaken her defenses.

Moving his tongue around in her mouth, he touched and tasted.

He was stirring emotions in her that she had tried to bury.

When her body started to relax, he knew that was a plus in his favor.

Milya forgot where she was. She longed for the feel of him, just like the dream she had.

Rick did not release his hold on her. While kissing her, he took both of her arms with his left hand and started relieving her of her blouse with his right hand. The trail of hot kisses led him to her breast.

Milya wanted to help him remove her clothes. The sensational feeling of his warm breath coming through the fabric of her bra to her breast sent the sexiest feeling she could remember through her body. Her nipples were taut.

This man was good. Not only were her pants down, but she was becoming damp by the movement being made with his fingers.

He released her hands as he rubbed her softly across her genitalia with his thumb, inserting it in and out with a circular motion. Leaving heat everywhere he touched her, he lightly kissed her vulva, never removing his thumb.

Her whole body clenched. Her muscles tightened around his thumb. He knew that he could take her to higher grounds, for he had prepared her body to detonate for him. Yet he wanted her climax to be felt with him inside her.

The transition went smoothly as he replaced his thumb with his manhood. He made sure that the entire tip of his penis was slick before he awakened her ultimate desire, by entering and withdrawing. With one jostle, Milya was withering beneath him.

She wondered what had become of the woman who didn't want this man? Knowing the answer to the question, Milya flexed her inner muscles drawing him deeper into her stream.

When their desires had been spent, Milya realized what she had done. She also remembered that she was still angry with him. "Get off of me!," Milya said through clenched teeth. "Remove yourself from me now!"

"Milya let me explain."

"I don't want to hear it. Let me up!"

Pushing with extra force, Milya made a maneuver that sent Rick sideways. "Never touch me again. I am too angry too deal with this right now," she said as she pulled up her clothes and arranged them neatly before she turned and stalked towards her mother's house.

Rick thought about chasing her again and making her listen, but decided against it. He knew that their next confrontation would only be a few hours away.

CHAPTER FIVE

"I don't think that she knows anything about what we want," the voice said. "I have been standing in the doorway observing her. She actually appears to be a weakling. I would have thought she'd put up a good fight, but she hasn't. It makes me sick to see women like that. Finishing her off should be easy."

Zaria could hear their voices and everything they said. She was determined to play the role of a weakling until an opportunity presented itself. She would then show them what a weakling could do.

Until that time came, she would do as she was told.

Steven and Katie McDougal arrived in the Delta around three thirty p.m. They rented a car and headed straight for Reba's house. It took them about twenty minutes to get there. Reba was sitting outside with Uncle Bennie when they arrived.

Steven let Katie out at Uncle Bennie's and parked the rental car at Reba's. Greetings and hugs were exchanged by everyone. "Where is Milya?" Katie asked.

"In the back of the house," Reba stated. "Why you wanna know?" Uncle Bennie asked.

"That's for me to know, Mr. Bennie, now tell me why you are so nosey?"

Before Katie knew what happened, Uncle Bennie had whipped out his knife. "I'll cut you. Gal don't make me cuss your ass out while I'm doing it."

"You are so right Mr. Bennie, look at you speaking like that to me. I forgot who I was talking to". Katie said to Bennie as she laughed.

"Bennie don't start on them, they just got here. Besides, we need to get your input on this disappearance," Reba was saying just as Steven approached.

"I told y'all that I could find that gal. She ain't missing, she's down there at them docks," Bennie was saying, but nobody heard him because Steven, Reba and Katie were all talking to each other.

"Mrs. Reba, has Milya seen Rick yet?" Steven asked.

"I think so because she stormed pass me in the house looking hot as cayenne pepper. I didn't bother her, and she didn't say anything to me."

"Well let's get this part over with," Steven suggested. "You know that she's going to be mad with all of us. I'll track Rick down, and the two of you go ahead and chat with her."

"I told y'all where she is," Bennie was saying, but before he could say another word, Reba cut him off.

"Bennie, Milya is in the house. Now come on and go with us and we'll wait on the others."

Reba, Bennie and Katie walked to the house and found Milya sitting at the kitchen table drinking milk with ice. They all shared a knowing glance at each other.

Milya jumped up from the table to embrace her friend when she saw Katie.

"Why didn't you call and tell me that you were coming?"

"Because I knew you would say that you really didn't want me to, when all along you would. Besides, I was worried to death about you, especially after that phone call you had."

"Where are your things? How long will you be staying? Where are the kids? Where is Steven?"

"For someone who was just sipping a glass of milk with ice, you sure are excited."

"Katie", Milya said taking a deep breath, "he's here."

"I know Milya. Our things are in the car, and we're staying the weekend just like you. The kids are at my mother's, and Steven went to find Rick."

"Rick, are you out here?". Steven was asking as he approached the first row of trees.

"Yeah."

"Where the fuck are you?"

"I'm walking towards you."

"How the hell are you?" Steven asked as he and Rick shook hands.

"In deeper trouble than I was before I talked to you."

"What could you have done since we talked earlier on the phone?" "Trust me, you don't want to know." "So you've seen Milya and the shit got ugly."

"That's the least of it," Rick said as he went on to tell Steven the non-descriptive version of what happened. The two men talked as they walked to Reba's house to join the others.

Reba waved her hand, signaling for Rick and Steven to enter the house just as they were about to knock on the door. "Come on in, the door is open," she said.

The atmosphere was explosive. Reba knew that she must be a buffer in this situation. She could tell that Milya looked strained, and she also knew that it had to do more with Rick than with finding or looking for Zaria.

"Would anyone like something to eat or drink?" Reba asked.

Katie was the first to respond. "No ma'am, we're here to brainstorm."

"Well let's all sit down so we can discuss the situation."

Milya looked at Katie strangely. Now she knew that something had provoked this spur of the moment visit. Katie cleared her throat, "uh-uh, Steven and I came down to lend Rick our support. We feel that the problems Zaria and Stan are mixed up in are life threatening. We know he has a lead on them, but we didn't want him to risk his life without your knowing it, and without our help."

Milya began to flex her fingers by opening and closing her hands. That the only sign of frustration that showed. It was obvious to everyone that she was. Then delete was she that at the end of the sentence.

Katie then went on to explain how Rick hired some people to track down Zaria, and how he was staying with Uncle Bennie to complete his investigation. All leads at this point were indicating that Zaria could be found in their town.

Milya's eyes widened with the last tidbit of information. She looked at her mother accusedly, "you knew all along?"

"Yes" was Reba's only reply.

"Oh, so that's why you were so sure I'd show up, and Uncle Bennie, you were in on it too. You could have said something. "

Milya's voice continued to raise the angrier she got. "I am mad! No, I am past that point. I'm tired of everyone treating me as if I were a two-year-old child!"

"Shut the fuck up gal. Folks trying to help you. Ain't no need for you to be hollin' at us cause you mad at that boy."

Milya's face discolored because she was indeed mad, hurt, confused and exhausted from her earlier extra-curricular activity. She hadn't had time to console her aching body.

"Stop bucking them eyes and get yourself together. The other gal y'all looking for is down at them docks, and we just got to go and get her. I got my knife." Every head in the room turned and looked at Uncle Bennie in surprise.

Rick asked, "Bennie, how did you know she was at the docks?"

"I saw her in that old car when I was riding my bike home from the senior citizen's luncheon at the boat."

"Why didn't you say something?" Steven inquired.

"Hell I tried to tell y' all, but y'all crazy asses wouldn't listen to me. She's with that other gal who likes laying on her back all of the time."

"Who is that?" Reba asked.

"Shit, I don't know her name, but she's always giving her tail away."

The five of them stood there staring at Uncle Bennie.

CHAPTER SIX

Plans were made to check out the docks. Everyone had a different strategy in mind, but Rick was pretty adamant about how things would go. The decision was made. As soon as the sun began to set, Rick and Steven would take a leisurely stroll down by the casinos.

"Rick, may I speak to you privately?" Milya asked.

"Sure," he replied.

She led him away from the kitchen to stand farther down the hall. "Rick, I appreciate what you're trying to do, but you don't have to. I'm capable of finding Zaria myself."

"Yes, I'm well aware of that."

Milya thought to herself, "why couldn't he just tell me that if something happened to me, he wouldn't want to live or just simply that he needs me."

"Rick, I'm going with you."

"No you are not," he said as he looked her. Didn't she get it. She was the reason he was willing to risk his life to save hers. He wanted no harm to come to her.

Milya was saying something about what she was going to do, but he didn't hear her because his mind had drifted. Abruptly he said, "Milya, you are not going with me and that's that. Dot, Dot, end of conversation." He embraced her and kissed her lightly on the lips. "I'll see you when I return, and then we'll discuss us." He left the room and joined the others in the kitchen.

Milya was steaming again. Of all the men in the world, why

did she have to hook up with him. She hated the way he tried to dismiss her by saying, "dot, dot, end of conversation," as if he was putting a period at the end of a sentence. Well, she would show him. She would give him enough time to get halfway to the boats before leaving to do her own searching.

Her composure was intact when she walked into the kitchen. Steven and Rick were leaving with Uncle Bennie to put the finishing touch on their plot just as she entered the room.

The girls looked at each other and knew what they must do.

After watching the three men leave, Milya, Katie and Reba sat at the kitchen table hatching a plan of their own. Reba said, "I know I can't talk you ladies out of whatever it is you will decide, but please be careful. This is serious business."

"We know mama. Katie and I will be extremely careful, and besides, we work well together."

"Mrs. Reba don't worry. We'll be back with Zaria before you know it."

"That's what I was afraid of. I knew the two of you would try to rescue Zaria the minute you found out where she might be," Reba said.

"Hold on Katie, we still have some unfinished business to discuss. When were you going to let me know what was going on?

I just remembered that I am mad with you." Milya stated.

"Girl, get a grip, or would you like for me to call Uncle Bennie. He can put you in your place. He's already shamed you one time today. Shall we make it two?"

"Yeah right, that's real funny. Anyway, what are we going to do? The people who have Zaria might try to shoot us if we get too close; we don't have any weapons."

"We don't need any. We will out smart them. I'm sure we know more about this area, with your help, than they do," Katie said.

"Well, I think that we should wait and let the men get a good head start," Milya suggested.

"You're right. You know that they will check to see if we are following them." Reba asked, "Then what? Are the two of you going to the levee?"

"Yes mom. We will dress in something dark from head to toe, then we'll go to the docks as if we were visiting the casino. We will act just like they do in the movies."

"Milya, I have one question. Is the levee and the docks the same place?"

"Yeah mama, the dock is just a name people call it because of the boats."

"Oh, I had to re-group. I kept thinking, where in the world is the dock?" The ladies laughed at that statement and began to get their strategies together.

Stan sat in a room surrounded by four people. He had been placed in a wheelchair with his hands tied behind his back. He had not been blindfolded, therefore, he recognized everyone in the room.

"Stan, we're only going to ask you once more. Where is it?", the interrogator asked.

"I don't know," Stan replied.

At that moment, Stan was hit hard in the face by one of his captors.

"That's not the answer we wanted to hear. You know what will sound sweet to our ears old boy, so sing it and sing it loud." "I don't know what you're looking for."

A punch in the stomach followed that response. Stan's stomach felt like it had closed around the person's fist, but he was not about to let his captors know that the last punch given hurt him to his soul.

"You know that we have your sister, and it's only a matter of time before we take her out if you do not cooperate. The answer you give us will determine whether she will leave here alive dear friend. Now let's try this again. Where is it? Ah Ah-Ah, think before you answer this time."

Stan had been trying to wiggle his hands free throughout his interrogation. He knew that GOD was on his side and his captors had made a grave error. For starters, they didn't tie his legs or ankles, and the wheels on the wheelchair were not locked.

The movement he had been making with his hands, loosened the ropes. His hands were almost free of confinement. He also knew that his sister's life was on the line, and he had a plan, a plan which was about to unfold.

It was just about dusk dark when Rick and Steven started getting impatient. Uncle Bennie was sitting on his sofa shaking his head at them. "I wish y'all would be still, you act like you're on fire."

"Uncle Bennie, when we leave here, don't let us look up and see you at the docks," Steven said.

"Yeah Bennie, your job is to make sure that the girls stay out of trouble."

"Both of you can hush up talking to me. I ain't doing shit. If I wanna go to the boats, I'm going; and If I wanna stay at home, I'm staying. I ain't watching no damn body."

"Uncle Bennie don't blow our scheme," Rick said.

"Y'all ain't got no scheme. I had to tell you where that gal was. I coulda' been had her if I weren't foolin' around with y'all jackasses."

Neither man said another word. They knew that they were fighting a losing battle. Uncle Bennie would do exactly what he wanted to do. The important thing now was to remain calm and keep a level head.

Rick looked at Steven and said, "let's get on the way."

It was a pleasant night out. Although it was partly cloudy, a few stars could be seen in the sky. Both men decided to wear dark denim jeans with a matching shirt and hiking boots. They said goodbye to the girls and Uncle Bennie with a stern warning not to follow them.

"For some reason I feel as if our warning didn't mean a thing, Rick." Steven said.

"I'm inclined to agree with you. Did you see the defiant looks on everyone's face."

"Yeah, I noticed. Timing is everything, so let's get this show on the road."

"How about that. Uninvited guest drop in and tell you how to run your operation.

Ain't that a bitch."

"Fuck you Rick. Like I said, let's roll." Rick and Steven left the house in the McDougal's rental car. The town was busy tonight. Maybe the casinos had an extra talent in the city that was drawing big crowds. Whatever the reason for the congestion, it was exactly what they needed to pull off their plan.

"OK what do you want me to do?" Steven asked.

"I don't want you to do anything right off. We will proceed to the casino and play a few hands of this and that, or a few slots. I will check with a couple of my associates, and then we will go from there."

"So in other words, you want me to sit tight until you tell me that it's ok for me to move."

"In other words, yeah."

"Now you know I don't like sitting around."

"Well that's tough. Let me ask you a question. Why is it that everyone that feels they have experience in the missing persons field? Ah-ha, just what I thought, you can't answer. I really want you to know one thing; this is not a simple walk in the park. This is some serious shit we are dealing with. One of us, if not both, could lose a life. I want you to be aware of what you're dealing with. Do you still want to go through with it.?"

"Hell yeah! I might make the ten o'clock news, you never know. I'm not stupid Rick. I know what risks we are taking. It's kinda scary, but I know that we are doing the right thing.

Zaria is a good person, and the girls would be hurt if they lost her. Where Katie is concerned, I'd fight all of her battles if I knew it would keep her from harm. She is part of me. Now let's get the job done. By the way, do you feel that this has something to do with the mob or drugs?"

Rick said, "I'll let you know more about it once we get there. To answer your question, this has nothing to do with either one."

The men drove the rest of the short distance in silence. Each involved in his own thoughts. People could be seen walking and talking up and down different streets of the town. Nothing looked suspicious or out of place.

The road on which they traveled was well used. Central Street was normally a busy street during the day. A school was located in the middle of the street. From eight o'clock in the morning until four o'clock in the afternoon, traffic flowed constantly. This street was also one of the avenues for reaching the docks. One could always find at least one vehicle on this road at any given time of the day or night. Tonight, the traffic was really hopping. Apparently the casinos were drawing a big crowd tonight.

"Katie, how long do think they have been gone?"

"About thirty minutes," she said. "That's all?" Milya questioned.

"Yeah. Waiting is the hardest part I think."

"Well, we'll give them about fifteen more minutes before we take off."

"I agree. I'm about to lose my mind."

Reba sat patiently waiting for the girls to make a decision as to when they should leave. She was anxious inside because she had a plan of her own.

"Would you girls like something to take with you on the adventure? Food, candy or maybe a drink?"

"No thank-you mama. We shouldn't be gone that long."

"OK, I was just checking."

"Katie, I can't take it anymore. Let's get started," Milya said.

"I'm with you. Let's do it."

The two of them left in Reba's car, because they sensed someone would recognize Milya's vehicle.

"Bennie, open the door. They're gone." "What ya knocking for? The door is open, brang your ass in."

"I'm not going to get into a game of tug of war with you. I just wanted to know if you are ready."

"I stay ready."

"Do you have your knife?"

"Hell yeah! I'm like that commercial, I never leave home without it."

Steven and Rick found a space to park the car. Proceeds from the casino in Greenville, Mississippi must be good from the looks of all other cars parked in the parking lot.

"Steven, let's go in and find a table or machine that is not occupied."

After securing the car, both men headed for The Sassy Duck Casino. People were moving from one casino to the other. As they approached, they noticed what seemed to be a larger number of security guards than usual.

The guards checked everything and everybody. They had never been checked when entering a casino boat before. That seemed very odd. Something was going on, and they would find out once they were on the boat.

Zaria knew that her time was ticking away. She had thought of every possible scenario. One of her thoughts was, if the kidnappers came into the room to collect the dishes, could she trip them with her feet and if so, how would she get away? Her hands were cuffed. She also thought about swinging at the person when they came in to adjust her handcuffs, but she remembered that she wore a blindfold. Would she be quick enough to remove them and swing?

Boy, she would have to move fast if she wanted any plan to work. She also knew that she could hold her own. She could take down at least one of them. Her brother had taught her how to defend herself when they were growing up. The problem was she didn't know how many of them there were.

Zaria had a lot of time to think. Being in that room was making her go crazy. She wondered if they had harmed her brother. She loved him with all her heart, but he was always getting into one trap or another. She prayed that he would be ok, but right now she had to worry about herself.

She didn't have long to worry about which plan she would

use because the door to the room opened, and she heard someone approaching.

"I hope you enjoyed the meal you had because it's all you will get until your brother cooperates further. Last I checked, he was barely alive" the voice said.

Zaria didn't respond. That statement pissed her off. She had to stay sane in order to defeat these people.

If her brother was hurt, then she was going to hurt someone.

Since she set the dishes aside, she could tell that they were being picked up. The plate and cup made a clacking sound as they were being gathered.

Zaria would not let them provoke her into doing or saying anything stupid. She felt that an opportunity would present itself soon, and she would be able to avenge herself.

"Are you as silly as your brother?" the voice asked. When she did not say a word, the voice said, "It is not wise to fuck with us. If you know where our possessions are, then I suggest that you tell us."

Zaria was given another minute to respond. When she didn't say anything, hands that felt like steel grabbed her around her arms and shook her hard.

"I'm trying not to kill you. Don't make me hurt you like I did your brother; I'm giving you one more chance. Do you know anything?"

When Zaria didn't respond the third time, she was hit hard across her face.

The impact of the blow caused her teeth to cut the inside of her jaw, but still she said nothing.

A second kidnapper said, "Leave her!

Let's work her brother over again. Once we kill him, we'll finish her. She will not leave here alive."

Zaria continued to sit still. She wanted to cry, but realized that there was no room for tears. She could hear their retreating footsteps. Then and only then did she silently exhale.

Uncle Bennie took his ten speed bike from the back room of his house and set it on the garret. He checked all of his riding equipment. He was also dressed in black, and he wore a utility belt that had multiple gadgets on it. James Bond would come to mind if one looked at Uncle Bennie now.

"Is everything in order old man?" Reba asked.

"I told you, I got your old man. I was born ready. You seen my pipe? I can't find it. I bought me some more tobacco to put in it."

"Your pipe is probably where you always leave it."

"Where is that?"

"On top of the toilet."

"You know, you're probably right. I did take me a good one this morning."

Uncle Bennie went into the house, retrieved his pipe, and walked back onto the porch. He lowered the bike onto the ground.

"Please be careful. If something happened to you, I wouldn't have anyone to argue with."

"I ain't going nowhere. I don't want you crying at my funeral 'cause y'all know you gonna miss me when I leave here."

"No one will cry at your funeral."

"Bull shit! y'all better."

Uncle Bennie put his pipe in his mouth, lowered his cap on his head, straddled his bike and paddled away. He waved at Reba and said, "I'll be back shortly. Cook something to eat 'cause I'll be hungry when I get back with that gal."

Reba watched him as he rode away. She didn't know what to do with herself but worry the entire time they would be gone.

In the meantime, she'd fry some ribs and bake a cake for Bennie.

CHAPTER SEVEN

Milya and Katie made their way to the docks, but they parked the car in the casino's designated parking space. They got out and casually strolled along the levee until they reached the area covered with sand. It could also be called the beach front along the great Mississippi River in Greenville, Mississippi.

This was the place where Reba's brothers and sisters swam in the Delta during the hot summers. This was also the same place Reba brought Milya, Zaria and their friends as well. They would feed the ducks from the river bank. Somedays, the girls would just sit and kick their feet in the water.

After walking a few feet, Milya said, "let's sit over by the trees so that we can take a look around and observe things."

"I agree, Katie said. We also need to make sure that we don't interfere with the guys. I have a feeling that we will run into them before the night is over."

"We don't have to see them. If my hunch is right, we will find Zaria and take her home before anyone gets hurt," Milya said with a smile.

They glanced over the levee. Two casinos, The Sassy Duck and The Glade House, graced the river banks. There were shacks on both sides of the river that appeared to be abandoned. Tall, medium and low weeds as well as grass grew around all sides of the shacks, but did not cover them completely.

"Katie, if I'm not mistaken, there should be an old bridge

around here somewhere that will take us from one side of the river to the other. The only problem is that I'm having trouble remembering where it is."

"Or whether the raggedly bridge still stands, "Katie said. "I have faith in you Milya because you once told me that no one knows the Delta like you do."

"I didn't know then that those words would come back to haunt me when I said that. Sure, every girl has wandered off at one time or another in her home town curious to find out what different things are out there. I am proud to say that when I was growing up, I was a very concerned and inquisitive citizen."

"That my friend, you still are. If you were not, we would not be down here looking for Zaria, and I could be at your mom's house eating some fried ribs. I know she will cook some before we leave."

"How, may I ask, do you know that?" "Because she knows Steven and I like them. Your mama can really cook!" "Sh', I hear something."

"What is it? I don't hear a thing."

"Don't move. Just sit by me and be quiet."

Steven and Rick casually walked around The Sassy Duck Casino. It was filled to capacity. There were a few slot machines open. A casino worker passed by pushing the change cart. Rick got twenty-five dollars in quarters. He knew that he would not get a chance to play them all, but he wanted to look involved.

Then on the other hand, it was to their advantage that the casino was filled wall to wall with people. Who could say whether they had been there the entire time if things got out of hand, and they needed an alibi. Another casino worker passed by them pushing a change cart. Steven stopped the lady and asked her for twenty dollars in quarters.

Once he was given the change, he and Rick found two empty slot machines that were side by side. Rick sat down at the two-coin Double Diamond quarter machine, while Steven sat at the three-coin Sizzling Seven machine.

They began to play, not really paying close attention to what they were doing. Rick was watching everyone, looking from one person to the other.

The doorbell rang several times before Reba could leave the bathroom and answer the door.

"Just a minute please." she said as she thought to herself, I don't like it when people constantly push that bell. Just ring it for God's sake and wait for someone to respond, that's what I say.

Actually, she was a little nervous about finding out who it could be on the other side of the door, with all that was going on this evening.

She looked through the peep hole and saw Sadie Monroe. Reba pulled the door open and presented Sadie with her warmest smile and said, "Hey girl, come on in," motioning for Sadie to come through the door.

"It's been a while since we've talked. Have a seat. Can I get you anything?"

"No thanks. I came to see you because I'm concerned."

Reba's expression changed from being a social hostess, to being puzzled. She had an idea what Sadie was going to say, but she wasn't sure if she would like the outcome especially if the news mentioned anyone being hurt.

Sadie said, "something is terribly wrong, and I'm not sure what it is. I do believe that something has happened to my children. I wanted to find out if you know anything. Zaria and Milya are so close; If Milya has told you something, please tell me."

"I'm not sure exactly what's going on, but you're right, something is wrong and both of our children are involved. Sadie, I think we need to pray."

Tears were forming in the corner of Sadie's eyes. It took her a minute to compose herself. The two ladies had known each other since their childhood.

They were involved in a lot of social events and functions because their children were around the same age and very good friends as well.

"Reba, I've called and left messages for Zarla, but all of my calls have been unanswered. She was supposed to be going to this conference, seminar or whatever it is for the college. I called her hotel number, but they said that she never checked in. I think that something bad has happened."

"Something is going on Sadie but what exactly, I don't know."

Reba could tell that Sadie was on the verge of breaking down, and she knew that she had to be strong for the both of them.

She didn't want to say any more than was necessary.

With a raised voice, Sadie said, "My sister is missing too!"

"Which one?" Reba asked.

"Jo," Sadie said. "She left yesterday and I haven't seen her since. At first I thought she may be at the boat, but now I'm not sure. The funny thing is, I don't know the best way to help them and it's eating me alive."

There was a vacant seat beside Rick. Someone sat down and put a token in the machine then replied, "They're not on either boat. We must check that area beyond the docks. There are several little houses that appear to be broken down shacks, but I'll bet otherwise."

"Good work," Rick said. "Let's go."

Rick gave Steven "the eye" as he got up. Steven followed his lead. As they walked through the crowd, both men knew that the action was about to begin.

They walked down past the Glade House Casino. People were mingling everywhere. There was a fishing boat about a mile down the river waiting for them.

"I was wondering how we would get across the river", Steven said in a whispered voice. "What's our plan?"

"We'll make it up as we go," Rick explained.

"You'd better stop Walter; I mean it. I'm not running after you anymore. We're already in trouble. Mama told us to be home an hour ago, but I wanted you to have fun in the sand, so we stayed longer. But that's it. Too many people are out here for you to go running off without me," one of the children playing in the area said.

"OK Veda, I'm sorry. Let's go".

Milya released a long sigh as she heard the retreating footsteps of what sounded like children-a sister and brother maybe. She didn't realize that the grasp of her hands was as tight as it was until she took that long awaited breath. Sand was beneath her fingernails.

She looked at Katie who was holding her wrist in a vise like grip and said, "You can turn me a loose now."

"Oh, girl I didn't realize that I had you. I must be out of my mind."

"Why would you say that?"

"Well since you asked, I'm sitting behind a tree, in the sand, holding my friend's wrist, and I'm whispering. On top of that, I realize that I'm scared shitless."

"Katie, we just had a little scare; now we know what it might be like while we're encountering the enemy. Are you ready?"

"Hell no! Let's leave this to the men."

"No! I'm going forward with or without your help. To be honest with you, I'm scared too. But Zaria is my friend, and I would like to think that if I were ever in trouble, she would do whatever it took to save me."

"Well I guess I'm ready now, but first let me say this little prayer. Lord, please don't let me die tonight or tomorrow. Help us please, because it is obvious that we are not too bright."

"Speak for yourself. Let's do this before we both lose our courage."

"Are you sure you know where this path is and where it takes you?"

"Yeah, we're right at it. It leads you to the other side of the river."

Weeds and grass were all along the river banks. In some areas, they both were almost as tall as the girls. There was a low breeze in the air which caused the grass to sway a little.

Katie followed Milya through the brush hoping that nothing drastic happen. They walked along a thick path that appeared to be well worn. Someone used it regularly. The indentations of the weeds suggested that someone had taken the time to push them heavily aside so that they would remain in that position along the path.

They walked slowly looking in all directions as they went. Halfway through the path, Milya stumbled and fell.

"Milya, are you alright?"

"Yea, I hurt my damn hand. What could I have tripped over?"

"I don't know. "What are you doing?" Katie asked.

"I'm trying to find the cause of my fall. It might be a clue."

Milya got on her knees and started moving her hands over the ground. In mid motion she stopped.

"What's wrong?", Katie asked.

"We have walked into some serious shit."

"What is it?" Katie asked as she knelt down beside Milya. When her hands came in contact with Milya's, she immediately jumped back and jerked her hand away.

"Dear GOD Milya! that's a person's body."

"Yeah, the question is whose?"

"Girl let's get the hell out of dodge."

"No wait! I have to see if it's Zaria.

The body had been half buried. A human hand from the wrist to the finger tips was sticking up out of the ground. The girls got two sticks and began digging the unknown body out of the ground. The top of the person's head was as far as they uncovered before gunfire split through the night air.

The three men sat in the boat attuned to everything around them. The waters were calm tonight as they neared the opposite shore. That in itself could be a problem each man thought, because it was also a little too calm on the other side of the river.

"Steven, watch your back. They know we're coming," Rick said.

"How do you know that?"

"I can just feel it. Something seems too peaceful tonight."

The men got out of the boat and pulled it mostly onto the sand. They left the tail end of the boat in the water just in case a hasty retreat was called for.

Rick scanned the area. He looked at the third man and said, "go and get the others, I think we'll need additional help tonight."

Rick and Steven approached the weeds. As they entered the tall grass, gunfire erupted.

Uncle Bennie rode his bike to the levee. There was a bridge located about a half mile down on the side of the boats. He paddled his bike until he could see the shacks. He slowed down, got off his bike, and decided to walk the rest of the distance to the shacks.

He heard gunfire. Uncle Bennie thought to himself, them damn kids done gone and got themselves caught. I bet I'm got to save them too.

He hid his bike in some of the taller weeds and turned it around so that it would be headed in the direction in which he came from.

He worked his way through the tall grass looking wildly around until he made it to the first shack. Everything looked peaceful, but then that was a sign to him that all was not what it seemed.

Uncle Bennie entered the first shack through a tinted, unlocked window. He waited for bells or a siren to go off, but nothing happened. The outside of the shacks were fake, a simple cover up or just a camouflage. In fact, this was not a shack at all. It was a state of the art government type building inside. Someone had put up and paid out a lot of money to make things appear as they were not.

On the inside, the floors were smooth concrete. Sheet rock had been placed on some of the walls. The walls had a sheen to them, almost blinding. The color appeared to be steel grey, and it gave off an eerie feeling, something similar to an asylum.

"These fuckers think they slick," Bennie said as he eased along the hallway.

The shacks were not small in size at all. Actually they were along the line of houses made in the early nineteen thirties, where the rooms were large.

He checked out several rooms by quietly opening the doors and scanning the area. It was obvious to him that the girl was not in this shack. He had to check out the others.

Just as he was about to ease one of the doors shut, something moved. He saw his attacker gaining ground on him. Using his peripheral vision, not wanting the person to know he was aware of his presence, he continued to be the careful snooper.

As this person charged at him, he gracefully avoided the attack. In one sudden motion, he had drawn his knife. The person turned toward him and said, "you better leave before you get hurt old man. I will give you a head start."

Uncle Bennie looked at his assailant and replied, "don't make me cut the funk from ya!"

"You've had your chance to stay alive old man, now you die."

But before the assailant knew what happened, Uncle Bennie had jumped toward the person in a semi-squatting position, cutting his attacker deeply on the thigh.

As the attacker instinctively reached for the cause of the pain, Uncle Bennie landed another powerful blow to the attacker's leg and head simultaneously.

Bennie's assailant body fell immediately to the floor.

After he put his knife away, Uncle Bennie said aloud, "I told 'em not to fuck with me, then I would'na had to hurt 'em." He bent over the body to pull the dark mask away from the person's face. Uncle Bennie shook his head and grunted, "he better be glad I didn't kill his ass," he said aloud. For he knew who the attacker was.

Milya yelled, "Run Katie!" as they both scrambled from the ground in an attempt to escape. Milya ran in the direction of the shacks, but Katie didn't follow. When Katie heard Milya screaming for her to run, she ran straight through the tall grass.

Milya headed for the second shack; but before she made it, something hit her in the back of the head-beside her left ear.

She felt something warm run down her neck, but she kept thinking, "I must keep running," right before she fell.

The last thought she had before total darkness over took her was, "this is the second time I've fallen flat on my face in the past couple of days, and was helpless. I hope Rick is nearby when I wake up this time too."

Someone walked up to her and kicked her on the shoulder, but she didn't move. "Let's take her inside. We may be able to use her to gain additional information."

Another person said, "I didn't want her shot; I wanted to use her as leverage, but no, you just had to get a shot off didn't you? I hope to GOD that she is not dead."

Zaria noticed that the band around her head was not tied as tightly as it originally was. Perhaps all of the moving about she had done, loosened it. It also occurred to her that the handcuffs she wore were not as secure as they should have been. In fact, they were not locked.

She wondered if she was being tested for some reason to see if she would fail or pass. If their goal was to see if she would take the bait, then they had reached it. She would try them on every turn. She then slipped her hands out of the cuffs.

When this was done, she waited to see if anyone would approach her. Nothing happened. She went on to take off the blindfold, but couldn't see a thing. She had to blink several times to adjust her eyes to the darkness of the room.

Finally she saw a light coming from underneath the door. That's when she realized that she was probably the only one without light. She wondered why exactly they wanted her. Figuring that would come out soon enough, she began to crawl around the room familiarizing herself with everything in her path. The iron cot, the wooden chair and the scissors she saw in the room, could be used for her defense.

She tried to open the door, but it was locked. She gathered the scissors and began to formulate a plan as she sat behind the door to wait.

CHAPTER EIGHT

The jarring of Milya's body awoke her. She felt groggy, and began to feel sharp pains. She also had a headache but didn't know why. Trying to figure out what happened was taxing on her brain, causing her some confusion as well as igniting additional aches throughout her body. Then it hit her all at once, the memory of what happened came back in a flash.

Milya realized that she was being carried over someone's shoulder. She tried to be perfectly still, not wanting to tip the enemy off that she was awake.

They approached the second shack. A couple of buttons were pressed, doors opened and they went inside. "Take her underground; we'll come and get her later," someone said.

As they approached the descending stair case, Milya opened her eyes just a little, so that she could see, remember and be able to retrace her steps.

She laid on the man's shoulder lifelessly. When they reached the bottom of the stairs, he took her to one of the many rooms in the underground. She prayed that he would just leave her and not tie her up; lo and behold, that's exactly what he did.

As soon as he laid her on the cot, a light siren went off- sounding something similar to a "morse-code". The man cursed and literally ran from the room.

Milya assumed whatever caused the man to leave her alone had to have been important. Her mind started to wander, and she began to get worried. She hoped that Katie was alright. If only they had stayed at the house with her mom, this wouldn't have happened. She also wondered if Rick and Steven were alright.

Milya said to herself, "so much for the pity party I'm throwing, enough is enough."

She sat up on the cot, but that was a bad mistake. Pain shot through her entire body, and she was forced to lie down again.

Rick and Steven dove for cover in the weeds. Rick looked around and saw one of the guys down that was with them. This was not the same man who had helped them paddle across the river. This was in fact another one of his associates.

A little bell went off inside his head just as Steven yelled, "Rick watch out!"

A guy dressed in dark clothing with a mask over his face, had a dagger in his hand. As he approached Rick, he said, "I've got your girl," then swung the dagger toward Rick's chest. Rick avoided the blow in the nick of time with the help of Steven's shout.

He stuck his legs out and came in contact with his attacker's feet, throwing the attacker off balance and causing him to land on his own dagger.

Rick looked at Steven and they both walked up to the injured assailant. After turning him over, they saw the blood oozing from the wound. The guy said, "You won't find her in time, neither one of them. If something happens to me, my men know what to do." Then his breathing became labored.

Rick frowned before he yanked the mask off of the guy's face. His eyes became as big as saucers as the realization hit him. This guy was one of the men with whom he had had contact throughout this whole ordeal. He realized that he and Steven had been set up.

This guy was "Big Dee's" little brother. Big Dee ran an auto shop in their town, that was one job among many. He was one of the guys that Rick had grown up with, and knew very well. He also had a knack for handling odd jobs for people, at a price of course.

Apparently, the younger brother was undermining his older

brother for some reason, or this could have simply been a trap all along. In any case, this was one of the worst nights of his life.

"Steven, let's get to the shacks and check them out. I think that my worst nightmare has come true. Milya and Katie have come looking for Zaria on their own."

"Dear GOD I hope not. Why do you say that?"

"This fool lying here said that they have my girl."

"Damn," Steven said. "They will not do right. If Katie has come here, providing that she is alright, I will give her a whipping she will never forget once this is over. I've never once, even thought of hitting my wife before. Let's go. The anticipation is killing me. Hey, will we leave this guy here?"

"Yeah, I'm sure his gang will find him. If he's hurt the girls, I want him to feel a taste of what it's going to be like for him."

The men walked in silence, really scoping the area. They didn't follow the ready-made path to the shacks; they made their own. Pushing weeds and grass away silently, they came to the clearing of the first shack.

Rick held his hand up for Steven to stop walking. He peered at the first shack. After about two minutes, he pointed in the direction of the second shack.

They eased back into the brush and picked their way to the clearing of the second shack. Again, they halted and stared.

Softly Rick said, "this is the one. I think they are expecting us or someone, so be on guard."

"I got ya, but heaven help them if they've got my wife."

"No, heaven help them if they've got Milya."

The two men nodded at each other and proceeded to inch their way to a side door that appeared to be slightly ajar.

"Let's not keep them waiting since they're expecting us. You got your shit ready and full of ammunition?"

"Yeah."

Gaining entrance was not as hard as they had anticipated.

Apparently something had already taken place and people had obviously left in a hurry or they were in another part of the shack. Perhaps they were at the other two buildings.

Rick whispered in Steven's ear, "whoever you find first, get them out of here and to Reba's house where it's safe. Be assured that I won't leave here without the others."

Steven nodded as they ventured off in different directions.

In the main office of the second shack, people were gathered around a desk talking. One man said, "This shit is getting ugly. If Big Dee finds out that we tried to do a number on him, we're all dead. Where the hell is Frank? Is he or is he not running this operation?"

"He's not here and hasn't been seen for a while. I'm going to tell you what we're gonna do," said a man called Little John.

"We're gonna have to clean up this mess before it reaches the big bosses' ears. Eliminate the guy and his sister and that should take care of any outsiders who could leak out the wrong thing."

Before he could finish talking, a younger guy who seemed to be in his middle twenties said, "We've caught two other ladies."

Everybody turned to look at the young man who was staring right back at them. He continued, "they were snooping around the shacks when we saw them. Then Boopie here, "pointing to the man next to him, got a little excited about seeing beautiful women and accidentally shot one of them."

Noise erupted from the room. There were about fifteen of them and they were all talking at the same time.

"Hold up, hold up!" the young man said. "She is not hurt badly."

"What the hell do you mean she is not hurt badly? Is she, or is she not hurt?" Little John asked.

"Well, if you let me finish, I might can tell y'all dumb asses."

"Shoot, Young Gun, and while you're shooting your mouth, be careful, because you could become a victim."

The two men stared at each other before the young man continued. "As I was saying, I brought the lady here and deposited her in one of the rooms below."

"Why'd you do that?," Little John interjected again.

"Because I didn't know if Frank wanted her or not. It's obvious she knows something, or she wouldn't have been snooping. Anyway as soon as I her to the room, a siren went off and I dropped her to come and see what the emergency was."

"I pulled the siren," Little John said, because one of our men was hit in Shack One. When I found him he was out cold. He barely came to and told me to watch out for the old man."

"Is he dead?" everyone asked simultaneously.

"No, but he's out of commission for a while. In the meantime, we need to search the buildings and grounds. Kill, bury and clean up things. Then we will leave this city and head back up state. Half of you go with Young Gun here and search the grounds, and half of you come with me. From there we will divide into four groups and continue."

"Hold up Little John," Young Gun said.

"The other lady ran in another direction, but I put somebody on her."

"OK, we'll get her. Let's get going."

Rick saw what he thought to be a concealed stairway that led below. He was right. This place had a basement in it. He was surprised that he hadn't come into contact with anyone.

He was as quiet as a mouse, streaking down the stairs. Actually, it reminded him of how he obtained the talents he has. Rick grew up in the hood where fighting was second nature.

He had to fight in order to get to school most days during his elementary years. He also had to fight in school and fight to get home. Some children were in different gangs and they would pressure other kids for their shoes, clothes, coats and hats even.

All of that roughness made him tough and hard. He had agility, he worked out and he practiced different martial arts. With age and growth, came power and skills. They didn't fool with him anymore because he was a force to reckon with. That's how he knew most of the crooked people around his town, because he grew up with them. He went on to college and advanced, and they became great at whatever trades they had.

Rick forced himself to bring his mind back to the present problem. He pushed open the fourth door and shook his head, because he had already glanced in and checked out three rooms while his mind was reminiscing.

Just as he was about to close the door to the fourth room, he saw a shape in the bed. Immediately he recognized her body.

Walking carefully, he checked out the room. His heart was beating frantically. He did not want her to be hurt. When he reached her, he put his hand on her shoulder, shaking her gently.

That's when she bit him. Trying to free his hand from her mouth, he had to grab her neck with his other hand and repeatedly call her name. He realized that she was terrified.

It hit her about the fifth time she heard her name being called, it was Rick. He was there to save her, or someone who sounded just like him. She was concentrating on biting the person so hard that she didn't open her eyes to see who it was until his voice registered.

She opened her eyes and let go of his hand. Blinking back tears of joy and relief, she just stared into his eyes.

He swooped her up in his arms and held her tightly not saying a word for a moment. Then he whispered, "what the hell are you doing here? Where is Katie? Why can't you just do as I ask you for once?"

All she could say was, "I don't know," as she held on to him for dear life.

He noticed that there was blood on the side of her face. "What happened to you? Are you alright?"

"I think I was shot in my head. It feels like I'm gonna faint. The pressure is awesome. I feel like I'm dying."

He checked out her face and realized that it was only a flesh wound. "You won't die until I send you to the great beyond after this, now let's get out of here."

"Rick I don't think I can make it. I feel weak, but believe me I'm damn sure going to try."

He looked at her and held her tight again. He was thinking to himself that when this is over, he was really going to have that long awaited talk with her. After he talked with her, she would never leave or take a break from him again. He would make sure of it.

He realized at that moment that life is too precious not to be with the one you love over simple and silly mistakes. The funny thing is that one doesn't realize it until it's almost too late.

Noise from somewhere outside of the room brought his attention back to the sticky situation they were in. He set Milya away from him and asked, "Do you think you can stand up?"

She nodded. They both stood and Rick waited for Milya to gain her stability. By then, she could also hear the voices in the hallway.

"Milya, things will probably get out of hand once we leave the safety of this room. Promise me that whatever happens, you will run and you will not stop until you've reached your mother's house."

"I'm not leaving you!" she said with such defiance.

"We don't have time to debate; our time is up."

As soon as he finished that statement, he heard someone say, "I'll check this end, and y'all go ahead and start on the next level."

Rick grabbed Milya and pushed her behind the door just before it opened. He stood to the right of the opened door. The man who entered never got a chance to see what happened. Rick delivered punches swiftly and quietly.

As soon as the guy pushed the door open, he entered the room without checking it out completely. Immediately he walked into Rick's fist. Caught off guard, the man staggered and Rick forced a blow to his juggler, cutting off his breath. Rick caught him and laid him down on the floor before giving him a final blow to the head. He wanted to reassure himself that this guy would not attack them as they left the room.

Milya looked at him with growing admiration as she watched the whole incident. She actually was amazed at how physically fit her man was. She knew he was in shape, but she had no idea of how much until that very moment. It surprised her that she was not afraid; for she was even ready to throw in her karate kick if it became necessary. She would not sit by and watch her man get hurt badly.

Rick asked her, "Are you ready? We need to leave before the next happy camper comes along."

"I'm ready to go," she said.

She actually still felt a little woozy, and pain was shooting throughout her entire body, but she was willing to give a hundred and ten percent to help save both of their lives.

Even though she was not at her best, she felt sure she could still bite, scratch, kick and holler. Whatever it took, she was going to do it. For the first time, she realized that her male companion had skills, and to help out, she decided that she would use the skills she had.

Rick opened the door to a lighted hallway, scoped the halls for movement and listened for sounds. He couldn't see or hear a thing.

He held Milya's hand and eased out into the hallway. He looked at her and said, stay as close behind me as you can, and then he walked briskly away.

Milya nodded her understanding and got right on the heels of his shoes. She didn't know that it would be so hard to function from having a simple flesh wound.

As they ascended the stairs, three men met them on their way down to check out the area. That's when total chaos erupted. A number of things were happening all at once.

CHAPTER NINE

Steven took a chance and exited the shack to search the grounds. His temper exploded at the sight laid before him. Just outside of the clearing, a little distance from the second shack, he saw a group of men gathered around something that took their undivided attention. Unnoticed, he positioned himself where he could get a better view of what they saw.

He saw his wife being forced to lay down on the ground with men surrounding her. One man was sitting astride her with his hands fondling her breast, and another one was holding her legs apart.

The top of her shirt had been torn. Her pants were half way her calves. The sight of this was sickening to Steven.

He entered the brush like a man on a mission. Firing and picking them off like flies. They were so engrossed with having a little fun with Katie until they were totally caught off guard. Some of the men had even put down their weapons to enjoy the sport.

They jumped as Steven charged in. He immediately took three of them out, aiming directly for their chests. There were five of them in all, two of which had a chance to regroup and counter attack.

Steven saw them trying to retrieve their weapons, and he shot in that general direction missing both of the men. One man turned and ran straight towards Steven. At that very moment, his gun jammed.

Stan made everyone in the room jump in surprise as he leaped from the chair he was supposed to be tied to. He grabbed the closest person to him, and that was Bethany.

She was presumed to be his female companion, but the agency

he worked for had ill feelings about her. He sincerely didn't want their suspicions about her to be true. He actually had developed some feelings for her.

"Get the fuck back, or this bitch is dead," Stan said.

People were slow to move so Stan shot the closest guy to him in the shoulder to prove his point, causing the guy to ball over in pain.

"Move back!" Bethany shouted. "We don't want to provoke Mr. Monroe.

"You're got damn right." Stan replied. He noticed the roaming eyes of everyone in the room, and he knew people were looking for objects or weapons they could use against him. "Now since everyone wanted to talk to me, let's talk. What is it again your gang wants to know Bethany?"

She turned her head toward him and stared at him real hard. If looks could kill, Stan knew that he would be dead by now.

Bethany replied, "Don't be a sour puss because I don't want you. It's nothing personal. Business is business. You have something we want, and I was sent to retrieve it by any means necessary. It's as simple as that. Now will you let these people go. It's me you really want."

"Well, I'm glad we've cleared that up."

Stan said. "Now stand back against the wall. All of you!" he yelled. "You've got to think of me as being a very stupid man Bethany, and that hurts."

He knew that he had to make a hasty exit, and he also knew that he had to take Bethany with him for security purposes.

He edged backwards holding her in front of him until he came in contact with the door. He made her reach around him to twist the door knob until it unfastened. Stan never took his eyes off the people gathered in the room, nor did he relax his hold on Bethany.

As soon as they were on the opposite side of the door, he fired his gun, shooting a hole in the bottom of the door. This was another scare tactic in order to assure his fast getaway.

He grabbed Bethany and began running, dragging her along

with him in the process.

The men charged down the stairs with knives drawn, swinging their hands and arms as they ran. Milya didn't know what to do first, or which way to turn. She bucked her eyes and prepared her body for battle.

Rick tripped the first guy causing him to stumble and fall down the stairs. When he lost his balance, he reached out and seized Milya, and they fell together.

They hit the bottom stair and floor with a bang. Milya didn't have time to concentrate on the pain sprouting forth throughout her body because an arm closed around her shoulders tightly.

She wiggled free from his grasp and somehow jumped on his back. Just before he tried to sling her off him, Milya bit down hard on his shoulder.

The man yelled, "Ouch bitch, turn me a loose!"

Milya sank her teeth further into the man's skin. He ran backwards banging her body against the wall over and over again. He was sure this would knock her off him.

There would be no such luck for this man. The impact from the contact of her body hitting the wall caused Milya to bite even harder. Blood was flowing from the teeth imprints in his shoulder like a three-inch open wound.

The pain was so severe to Milya that she closed her eyes and held on for dear life. The guy then jutted down the hall as if he were on fire. He ran around a corner and down another flight of stairs. He did not stop until he reached a semi opened door.

He was about to crash into the door, when it suddenly stood agape. Throwing him off balance once more, this little trek ended with Milya on the bottom again.

She landed with a thump and laid motionless on the floor. A chair hit the man in the back of the head before he had a chance to straighten up, rendering him unconscious.

Uncle Bennie said, "I knew I was gonna have to save her ass too.

Gal, come here and help me check this heifer out."

"Yes sir," Zaria replied.

They both searched Milya's body looking for wounds, cuts and abrasions. None were severely found except for the evidence of her head injury.

"She's got a pulse, so she's still alive. It ain't beating strong though. So let's get her out of here. She'll be out for a while though. Get her arm on that side and I'll lift her on this side, and we'll carry her together."

"Uncle Bennie," Zaria called.

"What!" he answered.

"I can't leave my brother."

"The hell you say. You gonna leave his ass tonight. Stop looking worried child. I'll come back once y'all are safe, now let's go."

Steven found himself in what appeared to be a bad situation. Two guys were closing in on him for the kill. An all-out brawl started. Licks were being passed, but no one was falling.

One guy tried to dive and tackle Steven's legs, but Steven was already falling. So when the guy leaned forward to grab Steven, he hit nothing but grass and dirt.

That gave Steven the perfect opportunity to fall and roll over. He stood quickly and kicked the fallen guy in the side, causing him to grab his ribs in pain.

Steven continued to rough this guy up. When all movement ceased from him, Steven searched for the other one. The second guy held Katie at gun point.

She looked at her husband and begged him with pleading eyes not to do anything irrational. Steven walked towards both of them slowly.

"Stop mister, if you value your life as well as hers, you won't come any closer."

"No mister, it's you who should be afraid. Your life means nothing to me. Let the lady go."

Steven never stopped walking towards them, and Katie had a look of dismay on her face. Her appearance was rugged. Her hair was wind blown and all over her head. The shirt she wore had been torn exposing some of her breast, and her pants were still straddled her legs.

Katie was certain her husband would get himself killed, and she was not about to let that happen. Steven was only a few feet away from them when she elbowed the gunman in the balls. The impact from the punch caused the man to turn her a loose and grab his private parts.

Steven did not wait for a better opportunity, he pounced on their attacker forcing Katie to fall backwards on her bottom. Steven had the upper hand. It was obvious that the man was in pain, but that did not stop him from stabbing Steven in his left shoulder. He succeeded in dragging the knife down his arm before Steven got a hold of the man's hand forcing him to drop the knife.

A numbing sensation was becoming evident in Steven's arm. He did not let it keep him from kicking the guy in the chin.

Katie found one of the guns that was on the ground and held it steady as she pulled the trigger aiming at the fellow's body. She tried not to hit her husband as he wrestled with the guy on the ground.

Pow!! was the sound one heard. Then she saw the two bodies lying motionless in the dirt.

"My GOD Steven, please say something."

Katie screamed as she ran to her husband's side. She was fearful that she'd shot the wrong man.

He didn't move. He waited until she was right upon him before he grabbed her pants that were still down around the lower part of her legs.

She fell across his legs and Steven said, "since your ass is turned up, I owe you something." He began spanking her for causing him to worry. He gave her five licks on her butt and explained why each lick was given. She wiggled as he administered his whipping.

"Katie, don't you ever go off risking your life again. The kids, your parents, sisters and brothers need you. Most of all Katie, I need and love you very, very much."

He sat her away from him and snatched the knife out of his arm. Blood started to flow like a fountain.

"Katie, why in the hell did you come out here?"

Shocked by what her husband had just done to her and becoming angrier by the minute that he sat there bleeding like a pig fussing at her, Katie pulled her pants up, and fixed her shirt as best as she could before she said, "Baby please let me explain."

"No, look at yourself. You were half naked and have shown unknown men your, no I take that back, My Gold."

"Wait a minute dear husband. This may well be "your gold" as you put it, but the Good Lord gave it to me before I shared it with you. I know it was a little risky coming here, but Milya and I were just as concerned as the two of you were about Zaria."

Katie was talking extremely fast because by this time, she was mad and was actually steaming that he called himself whipping her.

"Oh dear Lord Steven. I forgot about Milya. I was so caught in my own problem that I truly forgot about her. I have to go and find her."

Gunfire erupted nearby and blasting sounds could be heard. Steven said, "we'll discuss this later. Right now, we have to leave here before something else happens."

Stan gained access to another open door that led to the outside. It actually looked like a war was going on. There was gunfire exchange and different group fighting taking place. He stopped running and slowed his pace down to a semi brisk walk.

He said, "don't make a scene Bethany, and I won't have to hurt you."

The first weeds they came upon, he walked directly into them, trying to force her along with him. She was beginning to make a scene herself, hoping she could draw attention to them.

It worked. One guy did see them and automatically shot in their direction. Stan dropped Bethany's arm and made a dash for better cover.

Sticks and tall grass cut his face, legs and arms as he ran. His plan was to lose them and then double back. He had to find his sister in all of that mess. He was not going home without her.

He could hear shouting all around him, and he knew that some unnecessary roughness was going on. He prayed that nothing bad had happened to Zaria.

As he ran, he looked over his shoulder to see if Bethany or anyone else for that matter followed him. He didn't see a soul.

"Good, this will give me time to catch my breath," He said as he slowed down enough to get his bearings.

When he turned back around to observe his location, he heard someone say, "Burn him and those weeds down, all of them. If you see something move, shoot to kill."

That was all he heard. At that very moment, something hit him in the head, and he lost consciousness.

CHAPTER TEN

Rick was fighting with everything he had. He looked for Milya between every punch he made. When he didn't see her, he nearly lost his mind. He was attacking every and anything in his sight. His only goal was to find his girl.

A siren went off and someone yelled, "Pull up and pull out. The cops are on the way. One, Two, and Three will be blown to pieces in less than five minutes. Let's roll!"

Just as fast as the fighting started, it broke up. People were scurrying everywhere. The guy closest to Rick kicked him in the groin before he fled, causing Rick to stumble. Rick got up slowly, but instead of following the guys out, he searched the halls and rooms for her.

"Milya! Milya!" he yelled louder and louder each time. Calling her name over and over again. He never got a response. Smoke started to fill the hallways and he assumed they were setting the buildings on fire. He still had time to search for her. He couldn't leave without her. He just couldn't.

Not giving up the search for Milya, he went on to look in rooms down the next staircase. He found a room that was locked. He was convinced that they had somehow put Milya's body in that room. The door slung open with one kick. Looking wide eyed, he scanned the room in it's entirety with one glance over it. She was not there, but there was another door in this room. As soon as he opened it, explosives went off.

The blast was felt for miles around.

Police cars as well as rescue trucks and firemen had to stop. The vibrations were very strong. There were cries of hurt and pain as well as furor from people wanting to assist in whatever way they could.

"How is she Doc."

"She looks a little worse for wear. She's shaken up a bit and she's lost quite a bit of blood, but she'll live. She'll also need plenty of rest and relaxation, even though she'll say she's fine or feels better, don't let her stir too much. We'll have to watch those headaches she's going to have and see if they cause her any problems."

"Thank you for coming out at this late hour Dr Dale. We really appreciate it."

"Now Reba you know that I have been servicing this family a long time. That's what friends are for. Oh, don't forget to give her these pills and put a little of this liquid in her water for pain when she wakes up. I'll be back tomorrow to check on her. If she has any significant problems tonight, call me. See y'all later, and by the way, I want an explanation."

"Wait Doc! I have two others here you need to see."

"What the hell happened?" the doctor asked.

"I'll tell you later. Right now I need your expertise."

Reba knocked on a door before they entered.

"Come on in Mrs. Reba," both Steven and Katie said.

She opened the door and allowed the doctor to enter first, and she followed.

"Hi" Steven tried to say spryly.

"No, the question is, how are the two of you?" Reba said.

The doctor walked towards the gentleman lying in the bed. He pulled the blanket back and began his examination. Katie was hovering nearby. She had really been shaken up.

"Reba, this wound is bound to become infected if we don't get some medication into this man now."

"Do what you have to do doc," Katie said.

"Are you his wife?" the doctor asked. "Yes I am." she responded.

"Do you mind stepping outside of the room for a minute?" the doctor asked.

"Yes I do. I don't mean you any disrespect doc, but I don't have a weak stomach. I can handle whatever it is that need to be done."

"Very well then, help Reba restrain him. I'll have to clean the cut up a tad bit so I can see what's really going on. He's half out of it, but he will feel some of what I'm about to do."

"Son are you all right? Can you hear me son?" Sadie was asking sounding anxious.

"Hell, I didn't hit him that damn hard" Uncle Bennie said.

"Uncle Bennie, I just appreciate your help." Zaria said as she walked up to him and gave him a hug.

"I wasn't sure of what would happen to me."

"Gal I would a been done gotcha but these fools wouldn't listen to me."

"Hush up y'all, Stan is coming around."

"What's going on?" Stan asked.

"I stopped your sorry ass from getting killed. That's what happened."

"Mr. Bennie, why are you here?" Stan asked looking confused. He looked around the room for the first time and realized that he was not inside of his mother's home.

"Why are we at Mrs. Reba's house?" was Stan's second question. Then it hit him. He remembered what happened. Just as he was about to make his fast get away, something hit him in the head.

"Mr. Bennie, please tell me that it was not you who hit me in my head."

"Yes I did." Uncle Bennie said pointing his finger at Stan. "They was about to shoot you boy, but I didn't let'em. It was up to me to save you."

"Well, thank you Mr. Bennie. When I first woke up, I was disoriented. I didn't realize where I was nor could I figure out why I have this enormous headache. But that's all been solved for me now."

"Boy, I hope you ain't salty with me. Cause I'll do something your mama ain't done in a long time. Shit, you thank them other men was gonna getcha, I'll tear your ass up."

"No, No Mr. Bennie I didn't mean it like that." Stan jumped off the sofa as if he had just remembered something. He grabbed his head in the process as he stood making preparations to leave the house.

"Son, where are you going?"

"I'm going to get Zaria. They have her in one of those shacks."

"No they don't brother, I'm right here."

Stan turned at the sound of his sister's voice. The sudden motion made his head swirl. He had to steady himself by holding onto Zaria. She had made it by his side in time to help him. Pain and relief was written all over his face.

"Sit down Stan before you fall out."

Zaria cautioned.

"I believe I will. Mr. Bennie, what did you hit me with, a gun?"

"I did. Right cross the back of your head."

"I believe you too." "Why shouldn't you?"

"Ok, Ok, I see everyone here is on the road to recovery." Reba said as she entered the front room.

"I'm so nervous, I forgot that we prepared a meal earlier. Sadie and I have been praying, singing and cooking, hoping the Lord heard each and every prayer. If you are hungry, there is food in the kitchen."

"Did you fry me some ribs and cook my cake like I asked you before I left?"

Uncle Bennie asked.

"We did and there's rice and gravy, peas and cornbread. Oh well, let me just say this, make yourself at home. I'm still too nervous to eat, and besides, I've got to go and check on Milya again to make sure that she's ok. Then we'll get together and discuss the whole thing."

"Milya, what's wrong with her?" Stan asked.

"Well she was in that mess with y all too." Sadie said

"Has anyone heard from Rick?" questioned Reba.

Everyone in the room looked gloomy but Stan. He was confused. They could only think the worse. If that wasn't bad enough, how would they ever tell Milya that he was gone forever. Waiting to hear from the police was a hard thing to do.

"I got a quick question.' Stan said.

"Was Rick there too?"

"Yes boy, and so was Steven and Katie." his mother said.

"Can someone tell me what happened?"

"In a second bro, but first I'm going to sit with Milya for a while. Mrs. Reba, you rest for a little bit. Now it's my turn" Zaria announced.

The ladies smiled at each other.

Zaria entered Milya's room. It was almost completely dark. There was a lamp on in the corner of the room, but the wattage was low. Zaria sat in the recliner near Milya' s bed and held her hand. She spoke to her in a low voice as tears slid down her face.

"Milya, I know you probably don't hear me, but I want you to know that I appreciate all you've done to find me. I realize that I didn't come clean with you up front, but I didn't think it would come to this. How did I know I'd be kidnapped. Anyway, I guess that's why we've been friends for so long because we could always detect problems with the other one and could always count on each other. I love you girl and I hope and pray that you will be alright."

Milya interrupted her by saying, "It would ease some of my pain if you quit squeezing my damn hand."

"Girl! you're awake"

"Yeah. I heard you when you came into the room."

"Why in the hell didn't you stop me. You let me go on and on. Shit you know I'm grateful."

"Don't talk too loud, my head still hurts pretty bad, and I can't open my eyes too wide right now so don't think that I'm ignoring you. It bothers me, and besides, I'm too groggy. I forced myself to stay awake and listen to your sad ass story."

"You heifer you. If you weren't hurt, I'd get you."

"Girl It's like I'm in and out. I feel sort of strange. I feel pain, but it's kind of in the back somewhere."

"Dr. Dale's been over here so it ain't no telling what he gave you."

"Is he still here?"

"Yes he is, and he will probably be here a while. Enough of that. Let me finish my say."

"Ok go ahead."

"Before you shocked me by being awake, I was saying that you did some courageous shit. I ain't gonna lie. I don't know if I would have gone looking for you, I'm not sure what would have happened. You've got some backbone girl."

Zaria could tell that Milya was drifting in and out so she said, "I'm gonna let you rest, but I'll be back in a few minutes."

"Zaria, where is Rick?"

"He's tending to some business, tying up loose ends."

"Stop lying. You haven't heard from him have you?"

"No we haven't."

"I've tried not to cry throughout this whole ordeal, but If something happened to him, I'll probably fall to pieces."

"Don't think like that."

"I can't help it. It's all I can think about when I'm awake. I got this ache that won't go away."

"I know it won't, you got shot fool."

"You know what I mean Zaria."

"Yeah I know. It's going to be alright.

Worrying will not help the situation.

Let's just continue to pray. Please try to get some rest, or you'll start me to worrying. Once I start, Mrs. Reba, Katie and everyone else will start to lose it."

"You know what, I'm too weary, tired and sick to worry about anything right now. I'm sleepy."

"I know. You can see it in your droopy eyes. Please try to get some rest now."

"I will. I'm drifting now and can't keep my eyes open."

Zaria hugged her friend and left the room to join the others.

The Greenville police department was getting calls from everywhere. The explosions that took place by the river caused problems for the citizens who lived on that side. Ironically, the casinos continued to float and remain in place. The boats as well as the people aboard them were literally unharmed.

The Greenvillians only felt small movements from the incident. The explosion was something similar to a very minor earthquake. But on the other hand, the people who lived across the river received greater damage.

Fires were burning out of control. All gunfire had ceased. The dry weather in the Delta contributed to the problems they were having. It could reek havoc on its surroundings sometimes. Because when it's hot, it's hot.

The weeds and grass were dry. That was just the right elements for a seasonal fire. It hadn't rained in days. The ground was cracked due to the extreme heat. Smoke and fire was all that could be seen.

Reinforcements were called in to try and help contain the situation. Law officials from all walks of the government were there poking around. The towns people were getting suspicious.

Road blocks were set up around the general area. People were being turned around. No one could gain entry into that section of town.

"Hey, hey! Let's get some help over here. Get those people back."

As orders were being carried out, the man who gave them slipped through the crowd, and away from the disruptive scene. He tried to figure out the best route back to Uncle Bennie's house. His first thought was to check and see if the car was still parked in front of the casino.

There would be no such luck. It was gone. Apparently Steven

had taken it back to Mrs. Reba's house. His only other alternative was to walk the necessary blocks needed to get there.

He was amazed that he was still alive. While he walked, he thanked GOD for life itself. Although he was in pain emotionally and physically, he was alive.

After he opened the last door, explosives went off, knocking him further into a cellar, while forcing the door closed behind him. He stayed there for a few minutes then fought with the door to get out.

When he opened the door, blazes and smoke was everywhere. Rescue workers along with the boys in blue and black were also snooping about. To keep everything anonymous, he took a jacket off one of the firetrucks and began to be a part of the crew. He thought this disguise would help him search for Milya among the rubble unnoticed. He spent a couple of hours searching the grounds and the corpses, hoping to find a sign of what happened to her. Exhausted from worry and being weary, he decided to give up the search. When the time was right, he made his exit.

Now, all he could do was battle his heart and try not to fall down before he reached his destination. He did not want her to be dead. His whole reason for coming was to keep her out of trouble, but that was not to be.

He finally reached Uncle Bennie's house. He was given a key when he first arrived, so he entered the house without anyone's knowledge. His first reaction was to go to Mrs. Reba and tell her about what he thought happened to Milya. But he was not ready for that. Her body would have to be identified first before confirmation could be given.

He decided to slip through the back door. He would get a bath, change clothes, then deal with the others and reality. Upon entering the house, he passed by Uncle Bennie's famous liquor cabinet. He opened it immediately, snatched out a bottle of Hennessy, and drank heavily. The first swallow left a heated path throughout his entire body. Taking a deep breath, he forced his aching body to keep walking until he reached the bathroom.

He turned the water on, and let it run for a while. The steam it produced caused the mirrors to fog up. He had no use for them. He didn't want to see himself. He still couldn't give up hope that somehow Milya was still alive.

He stepped into the shower. The hot water felt good beating against his body. One would think he'd been in a boxing match. The soreness from this ordeal was beginning to set in, but the shower eased some of his pain.

Rick was really distraught. He had imagined a hundred ways Milya may have been killed. He would give up his life for hers in a heartbeat. If only he could see her once more.

He wanted to smell her, touch her, just simply be near her. There was an outside force so strong that he had to follow up on it.

Once the hot water soothed his body, he decided to dress in something cool and relaxing before he went to Reba's house and visit Milya's room.

The weather was extremely hot and muggy, sort of sticky like. The Delta was known for its heat and humidity during the summer months. He put on a t-shirt and a pair of cut-off blue jeans. Lacing up his running shoes, he left Uncle Bennie's house to find comfort in Milya's room.

As he stepped out of the house, a thought quickly entered his mind. It worked once, maybe it'll work again. He decided to enter her room again through the window. He was not ready to face anyone just yet. Why entering the house couldn't be done the correct way he didn't know. He wanted this time to be his, and his alone.

He reached her window and pushed it lightly. It moved with ease just as it did the first time. She was there before when he tried this, maybe she'll be there this time too.

Hoping against all odds, Rick crawled through the window and stopped once he made it on the inside. He looked outside to see if anyone saw him. Turning around, he stopped dead in his tracks. It was like seeing a mirage.

CHAPTER ELEVEN

Milya felt as if she'd been asleep for years. In her dream all she could do was call out to Rick. She wanted him like she'd wanted no other man.

Still groggy, she turned over on her side, reliving the dream she had a couple of nights before when she thought Rick was in her room making love to her.

"Rick," she said softly as she continued to dream.

Not being able to shake this mood in her present condition, she had to be content with sensing him, and mentally drawing him near to her.

At the sound of his name being called, Rick jerked his head up. He was happy, excited and relieved all at once. His woman was safe, and she wanted him.

He saw her turn over and realized that she was out of it. Apparently she was heavily medicated and dreaming. It was good for him to know that when she was out of her mind, he was still on her mind.

He thought out loud, "first things first."

He walked to the door and locked it, then he turned toward Milya. He had to check her out for himself. He walked over to the bed and touched her face with his hands. There was a bandage around her head. He kissed her there.

He gave her body a once over examination. Her arms and legs were scratched up a little bit, but they would not scar. He kissed every cut and abrasion she had.

She was dressed in a short, white, lacey night gown. It had thin straps across the shoulders and flared out to stop above the knees. The bodice was low cut with buttons that adorn the center of her nightie. She looked scrumptious.

He sat there staring at her for a while. Thanking GOD that she was alive, and she was his. Rubbing the side of her face gently with his hands caused her to turn her lips toward the inside of his palm.

He crawled onto the bed with her. Fire ignited in that very spot of his palm. He kissed her on the lips then, and she somewhat responded. That was more that he could bear. Sick or not, he had to have her.

He left a path of fiery kisses along her cheeks and neck. The moan that escaped her lips was barely audible, but he heard it anyway.

He kneaded one of her breasts with one hand, and he nibbled the other one with his mouth. Instantly her nipples perked up jutting pointedly. It was as if he were a starving man. He could not get enough of her; she was his life line.

He then took her hand and sucked on each of her fingers giving each of them the same amount of attention. Milya's moaning became a little stronger, but not loud enough to be heard outside the room.

Rick rubbed her across his most desired body part. She was already moist. He had to taste her there. He parted her legs gently and drank from her divine nectar. Her muscles contracted and she called out his name.

"Rick, you" re alive," Milya said in a weak voice. She was barely able to open her eyes.

Rick kept administering that marvelous feeling. Milya began to stir against his mouth.

"I want you inside of me now."

"Your wish is my every command."

He eased himself inside of her by slow degrees, letting her adjust to all him since it had been a while and she'd been hurt. That took more will power than he had. He saw himself losing control and tried to fight it, but the battle was lost to both of them.

He told her to hold on, and they rose to higher heights together. All of their energy was exhausted. After rising and falling together, they laid on top of the rumpled sheets blissfully happy.

"Milya, did I hurt you? I kinda lost it for a minute."

"No, you gave me just what I needed." "Oh did I now?"

"Yep. I can't move a muscle."

"I'm sorry baby. This is the second time that I haven't made love to you properly."

"What do you mean?"

"I know you like the whole nine yards baby, but I didn't think your body was ready for that."

"You're right. I am entirely too sore."

"We have a lot to talk about. Let me get you cleaned up and get you a fresh gown. We can discuss all that's happened while I bathe you. Drink some water, it will make you feel better.

There was a soft knock at the door. "Just a second." Rick said softly.

He walked to the door and unlocked it. As he opened the door, his fingers were placed across his mouth, signaling for her to be quiet.

"Sh, she's sleeping, and she's very tired."

"I just bet she is," Katie said smiling. She entered the room, and they hugged each other. Rick closed the door behind her.

"Man, I'm glad to see you. We all thought you were dead. They are up front waiting for the police to contact them about you. I'll go tell them that you're ok."

"No, don't. I have to leave and tie up a few loose ends."

"Well I thought you had done that already before I came in."

"Shut up Katie. I want to let you know that you and Steven were truly brave to take the risk you took. I'll be back soon."

"Ah ah, don't say a word, I can see it in your face. We shouldn't have, but we did. And don't you go where Steven did.

He's already fussed enough at me for himself and for you."

"Well I guess I won't this time 'cause I know Steven spanked that ass, didn't he?"

"What?"

"You heard me."

"What do you think you know about that?"

"Katie, we were both scared shitless for the two of you, and besides, we love our women dearly. I've got to run. See yah." "Rick."

"Yeah." "Thanks."

Rick turned to leave the way he came in. "Why in the world are you leaving through the window?"

"Because it's the way I came in. Frankly it's none of your business though. By the way, let her sleep until I get back. She's had a busy day."

"I bet she has. Why don't you just jump on out."

Katie walked over to the bed and held Milya' s hand as she silently cried. She had never been involved in anything like this before in her entire life. It was truly terrifying.

Milya felt something and knew that someone was nearby, but she was unable to respond. Without her knowledge, Rick had slipped a little of the laudanum in her water glass that Dr. Dale left on the night stand by the bed. This was the cause of her deep sleep.

"Milya, I know you probably can't hear me, but I'm glad to know you are alright. We'll talk later and get all of the details straighten out."

Katie then left the room to go and check on her husband. She was weary and exhausted from the whole ordeal.

Rick managed to find the police station. He entered the building and sought out to find the chief's office. He wandered right into it. The police chief welcomed him into his office. While they were conversing, other authority figures came into the room.

Matt Benton was the head of special operations. He was among three of the men who entered the room and wanted to know what went on. Rick spent two hours at the station going over every detail of the events leading up to the day's actions.

Rick decided to take the four men with him to Mrs. Reba's

house so they could get all of the info they needed from everyone at one time; that would speed up the process and make things easier for everyone.

They left the station and followed each other to the parking lot, talking to one another as they went along. From there, Rick got in his car and lead the way. The other four men rode together.

Rick knew everyone would be surprised when they found out exactly what went on. They made it to Reba's house in about fifteen minutes, got out of their cars, walked up and rang the doorbell.

Reba answered the door, looking extremely happy that Rick was still alive.

"Rick!" She exclaimed as she gave him a motherly embrace, "boy we thought something bad had happened to you."

She then noticed that there were other people gathered at her door as well. "Pardon me, hello gentlemen."

They all returned her greeting at the same time.

"Mrs. Reba, these men need to ask a few questions about what went on today, and they need to talk to everyone including Uncle Bennie."

Before Reba could invite the men into her home, Uncle Bennie spoke out.

"Who the hell wants me?"

"Hush up Bennie." Reba said, looking at him harshly.

They all went into the house and Reba directed them to the den. Rick helped Steven to the room and sat him in a chair. He was still semi-groggy but coherent. Milya was sitting up in her bed when Rick strolled into her room, opened her closet, and pulled out her maroon robe and matching slippers.

"Mr., what are you doing, and where are we about to go may I ask?"

"In the den. The police chief and some agents want to know what happened. I just want to make sure that you are comfortable but not baring anything, if you know what I mean."

Milya smiled and allowed him to dress her for the interrogation. He worked fast, but efficiently. He then carried her, against her will, to the den.

"I wish you would put me down."

"I will now, but not later."

Rick placed Milya on her feet but not before everyone saw how well he was taking care of her. They were all in the den now, but Stan was still asleep in the recliner. He opened his eyes to the sound of the escalating noise around him.

"Mr. Benton, what are you doing here?", Stan asked while sitting up in his chair.

Everyone looked surprised that he even knew the men except Rick and Uncle Bennie.

"That's what I'm about to ask you. What in the, pardon me ladies, hell happened?" Matt asked. "Wait one minute Mr. Benton. Don't go yelling at my son," Sadie said.

"It's okay mom," Stan reassured her. "Matt and I know each other very well."

The chief of police stepped in then and introduced everyone in the room. Matt took over and started asking questions. He wanted to know when and how everyone got involved, starting with Milya. She told them what happened to her from the moment she arrived in Greenville, leaving out why she'd come in the first place.

Matt asked, "Why did you suspect that something was wrong Milya?" "Well Mr. Benton, it's not like Zaria to leave and not contact me."

"She's right about that," Zaria added butting in.

"Oh I see," was all that Matt said. "Milya, is this when you involved the McDougals?"

"Yes it was. I knew that something was wrong and I didn't want to upset our parents, so I called Steven and Katie."

"I see. Now is this when you invited them to join you in the search?"

"No!" Katie interrupted. "I talked with my husband, and we decided to check on Milya ourselves. She didn't know we were coming."

"Well now, I've heard enough of this bullshit," Uncle Bennie said. "This could take all night. What y'all need to ask is when that damn boy over there let things get out of hand and got his sister captured."

All heads and eyes turned towards him, and he stared directly at Matt, waiting on him to say something.

Matt said, "We'll get to that I grant you Mr. Bennie."

"Well shit, get to it."

Ignoring Bennie's last statement Matt said, "proceed Mrs. McDougal."

"Really Mr. Benton, there is nothing more to tell. We caught the plane and came here."

"I see. Now Zaria, how did you get captured?"

"It's a long story, but to sum it all up, Stan asked me to meet him in front of the old E.E. Bass Jr. High School. I thought that request was odd, but I went anyway. When I got there, I was in for a big surprise. Two goons were waiting for me. I hurt one of them, but the other one took me out. He hit me in the head with something."

Stan said, "they were holding her for insurance. Her phone line had been tapped, so they knew she was my sister because I made some calls from her house."

Reba and Sadie sat quietly through all of the questions. They would question their children once this little session was over. Uncle Bennie, on the other hand, began to get restless.

"Is this when the two of you proceeded to look for Zaria on your own?" Matt asked. Both ladies said "yes" in unison. Uncle Bennie shocked everyone again.

"Y' all need to tell 'em the truth. That gal he was liking set his ass up and almost got everybody else killed in the process."

"Enough!" Matt yell, causing the entire room to stare at him. "Will you ladies excuse us? I need to speak with the men of the group alone."

"I ain't scared of your big long lanky ass." Bennie said as he placed his hand on his knife.

"Calm down Bennie; we are all ready to go," Rick said.

"Then he needs to tell the truth. We all know that Stan works for them."

The ladies were leaving, but they all heard that. Zaria was the only one who knew that her brother did occasional undercover work, because he had just let her in on his little secret before she was kidnapped.

They left then and went into the kitchen where they could question one another.

Reba and Sadie immediately began to prepare simple snacks as they held their own interrogation. After asking them questions about the incident, Reba asked, "How are y' all really feeling Milya, Katie and Zaria?"

The girls agreed that they were ok, just a little tired. Milya was actually feeling better than she thought she would. "Dr. Dale must have given me some powerful stuff, because I'm not as lightheaded as I was earlier."

"That or Rick put some extra medicine in your water to make you rest longer," Katie said.

"Knowing him, he probably did. I just wish I could hear what they were saying. It's beginning to get a little warm in here. Is the central air messing up again mama?"

"Yeah. I called the guy to come and take a look at it, but he can't come until tomorrow some time."

"That's good because the heat and I don't get along too well."

Everyone laughed at Milya's statement.

"Now that we have all calmed down, maybe we can finish gathering all of the necessary information needed for our records."

"Since the smoke screen has been lifted, why don't you go ahead and tell us the truth," Rick said.

"Stan is in our employ, and he is a darn good computer specialist who just happened to run across some additional info while on assignment," Matt said.

Matt and the police chief assembled all of the details needed to wrap up the case. The chief and two of the guys left, but Matt stayed behind.

"Where is it Stan?" Matt growled low enough so that only the four of them left in the room could hear him.

"It's in Milya's overnight bag where it's been all along."

"What?" Rick nearly shouted. "I know you didn't intentionally put my woman's life in danger. Did you lose your goddamn mind?"

"No, No, it was not like that."

"The hell it's not. She could have been killed for some bullshit she didn't even know about," Rick said as he restrained himself from hitting Stan.

"I thought it was Zaria's, anyway it looked like hers, the one she never takes out of the house. By the way, I had things under control."

"When?" Uncle Bennie asked. "You forgot that I had to save your sorry ass."

"Yeah Stan, and if that don't beat all, you got Katie mixed up in all of this as well. You know the girls love each other and would go to the end of the earth for one another.

That's why I'm pissed off with you, because Katie was almost raped. It tore my heart out to see a bunch of men standing around my wife like she was Sunday's dinner."

"Hey guys, I didn't know that Bethany was setting me up. I'm as upset as all of you, if not more, because it is my fault that all of this happened."

"Ok, that's enough brow beating. Let's all be thankful that everyone came out of this alive. Stan, go and get it so we can put it on lock down," Matt said.

Stan left the room and returned moments later with a tiny box. He handed it to Matt, who opened it and studied it's contents. Everyone else surveyed the box as well.

"There's this other matter we need to address while all of us are together, it concerns Bethany," Matt said.

By this time the ladies entered the room carrying trays filled with food and drinks.

Matt began to gather all of his material and placed them inside of his locked briefcase.

Reba said, "Since it so late Mr. Benton, you are more than welcome to spend the night here with us and then depart on tomorrow. I have already prepared a place for you to sleep."

Matt graciously accepted the offer. He was tired and hungry. Everyone had a hardy appetite by now. They all chatted for a while, and then the ladies excused themselves to retire for the night.

Stan whispered, "I'm glad they are gone because I've been wanting to ask about Bethany myself. Has she turned up anywhere?"

"No. Everyone is accounted for but her and a few of the guys that she ran with. She was not found at the scene, nor was she found among the burned corpses. We figure that they all ran up state somewhere."

"That's where you are wrong Matt. She has a vendetta against me. She'll turn up soon."

"Don't worry Stan, we'll come up with a plan. You should be safe for the rest of the night. We'll get you out of here and away from the girls tomorrow," Rick said.

CHAPTER TWELVE

Milya made her way back to her bedroom. It was important to her that she put up a good front for everyone. She did not want anyone to know she was in pain, but now, she was beginning to ache. She picked up the pain medication that Dr. Dale left on her nightstand and followed the directions for the prescribed medicine.

She decided to take a shower before going to bed. Milya turned on the hot water and let it run for a while. With the warmth in the house along with the steam from the shower, things were heating up. She gathered all of her body lotions. By now, she could feel the medication working as it was already making her feel better.

She closed the bathroom door lightly as she disrobed and got into the shower. Placing shower gel on her bath sponge, she proceeded to bathe, singing to herself with her eyes closed.

Rick entered Milya's room and heard the shower going. Once again, he thought it would be best if he locked her bedroom door. He eased the bathroom door open without making a sound, and stepped quietly inside. He took off his shoes, but kept what he was wearing on, as he smoothly got into the shower behind her enjoying the view.

Milya had her eyes closed but she thought she heard a noise. She opened her eyes and pulled the front of the shower curtain back, looking towards the door. She didn't see anything unusual, so she continued to do what she was doing, and started to hum again.

Rick placed a hand around her mouth, and put the other one around her waist. "Don't scream and don't move," he said.

Milya began to thrash about until his voice registered in her head. The sound was muffled, but she said, "Have you lost your damn mind. You scared the shit out of me."

"Do you remember what I told you once before about all of your moving about when you're next to me? It makes me hard as a rock."

Milya stopped moving around. She realized that Rick's clothes were drenched, and they were sticking to his body. She could feel him through his clothes.

"When I let go of your mouth, please do not scream at me or make a sound."

Milya nodded her understanding, but Rick did not let her go right then. The hand that was around her waist slid further down her body, not stopping until it touched her trimmed mane. He rubbed her gently across her secret garden. The back-and-forth motion stirred something deep within her.

He began to separate her folds and rub her around her lips, inserting and withdrawing his fingers as he did so. Milya began to move against his hand.

"Don't move, let me work it for you," he whispered.

Rick was so involved with what he was doing until he was caught by surprise when Milya made a fast maneuver. She turned around and faced him, pushing him to the back of the shower. She grabbed his face with both hands and brought it down to hers for a long and hard kiss.

As she kissed him, she let go of his face and let her fingers roam all over his body. She unfastened his pants and let them fall to the bottom of the tub. His manhood sprang forth. He allowed her to pull his shirt off. Once free of that, he bent his head and began to suckle her breast. She held his prize in her hands as he did so.

Milya moaned aloud, and Rick nearly spilled his seed right then and there. He picked her up and gently eased her down onto him, periodically lifting her up and down so that the slickness she produced would help her adjust to all of him.

Milya wrapped her legs around his waist as he arched his back and dove deeply within her. She met him with equal force, riding him like a true buckaroo. They both forgot about the running water as well as the pain they had endured.

Physically drained, they showered and then laid across her bed facing one another. With the air conditioner on the brink, the room was warmer than usual. Neither one of them wanted to put on clothes or cover up.

Rick looked at Milya's body admiring her unique design.

"Milya, you look scrumptious."

"Watch out now. I don't think you can handle any more of me this day."

"I'm ready, willing and able," Rick said. He was becoming aroused again by just looking at her. "You know, I could get use to this delta heat when it's coming from you."

"Ha."

"I'm serious, look at me," Rick said holding his arms out to her.

Milya saw the evidence of his wanting her, and she went willingly into his waiting arms. They talked as he held her and made love to her throughout the early morning.

Rick got up at sunrise and went back to Uncle Bennie's house. The weather was still hot and muggy. He thought he noticed something move when he was in route to the house, but after observing the neighborhood, he didn't recognize any unusual activity.

People were stirring about in Reba's house, getting dressed and preparing for the day ahead. Matt had to get Stan to safety, until Bethany's whereabouts could be accounted for.

Reba and Sadie cooked breakfast for everyone. Stan, Steven and Milya were feeling much better. They all conversed with one another as they sat and ate their food.

Reba opened the front door because she could hear Bennie and Rick talking outside. They sat on her front porch, full from the cereal, toast and bacon they had eaten.

Matt stood and said, "Stan, we had better get going."

"Ok, I'm ready. See y'all later guys."

Matt picked up his briefcase and said his goodbyes along with Stan. Milya decided to walk out with them so she could sit outside with Rick and Uncle Bennie. They opened the storm door and filed out talking to each other as they walked. Bethany jumped from behind a parked car, and fired a shot striking Stan in the chest.

It all happened so fast. Rick and Uncle Bennie saw her first. Rick sprinted towards Milya, tackling her and knocking her down to safety. Uncle Bennie retrieved his knife and slung it at Bethany hitting her in her right shoulder.

At the same time, Matt drew his pistol and shot Bethany in her left leg, the upper thigh region. Her gun fell, and she collapsed on the ground.

People were screaming and yelling. They all thought Stan was dead. Rick helped Milya up and made sure she was okay. Stan sat up and tried to catch his breath. Rick, Matt and Uncle Bennie walked over to Bethany to check out her condition.

Although Bethany was hurt, she was not dead. "I got his ass. You can do what you want with me; but I got him, and I'm satisfied." Bethany could not see Stan from where she was lying.

"I seriously doubt it lady. He was wearing a bullet proof vest," Matt said.

Bethany snatched the knife out of her arm with the last of her withering strength, and tried to run towards Stan. She never made it. Rick hit her on the back of her neck causing her to drop to her knees. Shortly afterward, she collapsed.

"I'll call for assistance," Matt said. "The sooner we get this taken care of the better."

Uncle Bennie grabbed his knife, and he and Rick walked back to Reba's house.

"Stan, I thought you were dead for a minute," Zaria said as she hugged him furiously.

"Whoa, take it easy. My chest is burning. This vest kept me alive. We figured she'd try something," Stan said trying to talk between each breath.

Bethany was taken to the hospital and worked on before they took her into custody. The interrogation she was given was rather harsh and intense. All of the missing pieces of the puzzle fell into place.

The woman Milya and Katie found in the grass by the casinos was Ms. Sadie's sister, Jo. She had gone to Zaria's house and unexpectantly ran into Bethany while the search for the goods was going on. Since they knew each other, Bethany felt the need to dispose of her. She and one of the gang members were the two people watching the house all along. They were listening to incoming and outgoing telephone calls while trying to trap Stan. That's how they knew Stan and Zaria were related.

Big Dee's brother Frank had been running this outside operation for about two years. He and Bethany hooked up and decided to have their own ring of illegal business dealings. They stole items from one of the oldest and richest families in the Delta and resold them to the highest bidder, for the most part.

Stan had the pleasure of transporting the Delta's most sought out treasure, and Bethany found out about it.

Her job was to get involved with him, and make sure that he would fall for her. She was to relieve him of his duty of being the protector and transporter of the valuable goods as well as assassinate him. But that all backfired when Milya, Katie, Steven, Rick and Uncle Bennie got mixed up in the situation.

Bethany was the only one that stood trial and was convicted. Frank's whereabouts were unknown. His body as well as several other individuals were never found.

Things eventually went back to being somewhat normal by the end of the summer. Everyone had healed physically following Dr. Dale's medical advice. Stan went on to work on another assignment that took him out of the country for three months. Zaria ended up teaching her own class for the summer, and Katie and Steven returned to their home.

Milya went back with Rick, who upon his insistence that she was not truly well, persuaded her to move in with him. She noticed as the days went by, her patience and attention span were very limited. It was not like her to be short with everyone, or feel like she did. She was normally an easy-going person, but she felt uneasy because of the rumors that were going around about Bethany's release from jail and Frank's search for them.

She was feeling odd, but was almost positive that she wasn't pregnant because she was on the pill. Of course she missed a few doing her ordeal in Greenville because she was kept sedated for a while, but she'd already had a period for the month.

Rick came home early one evening from work and suggested that they go visit her mother. He sensed her home sickness, and knew it would lift her spirits. Milya was excited about seeing her mom again. She wanted to discuss her situation with her mother so they could figure out what was wrong with her. She really didn't want to be mean to Rick, because he was going out of his way to be extra kind to her.

What she didn't know was that Rick had seen Bethany and figured it would only be a matter of time before she tried to pull off another stunt.

He wanted Milya to be safe and in familiar territory. He had also made plans to propose to her in front of her family and friends. The engagement ring had already been purchased and sized.

"Ok Rick, when do we leave?"

"Whenever you want to," he replied, not wanting to sound overly anxious. Actually, he was ready to leave right then.

"Well, I was thinking, tonight would be as good of time as any to leave. What do you say?"

"Sure darling. You know your every wish is my command," he said as he smiled and kissed her.

They began to pack for the trip home. Rick then went into his study and placed a call to Big Dee to let him know their plans. They had talked several times in person and on the phone concerning his brother, and the commotion that took place in the Delta. Plans were made, and they hung up.

In the bedroom, Milya called Katie and Zaria on her three-way to let them know about her trip. The girls were excited. Katie immediately began to make plans for her and her husband to meet them at Reba's.

"Katie," Zaria said.

"Yeah."

"Are the kids coming with y'all?"

"No. They are still with my parents. She thought it would be best if they stayed with her until the end of the summer. That way, we won't have to explain a lot of things about Steven's arm."

"That was good thinking on your mama's part," Milya said.

"Girls it's a blessing to have parents who can help you out and don't mind doing so when you need it," Katie stated.

They all agreed. Milya ended her conversation, finished packing what she thought she would need, and placed her things by the door. By this time, Rick was coming out of his study.

"I see that you are ready. Let me get the rest of my things, and we can be on our way."

CHAPTER THIRTEEN

They left and got on the road heading to Mississippi. About three hours later, Rick noticed someone following them. "Not closely, but he recognized a tail when he saw one." He sure hoped things were in place like he and the guys had discussed before they left.

When they got to Reba's, everyone else had made it. They were excited to see one another. Rick opened the car door to let Milya out.

"I knew it," Uncle Bennie said as he jumped down off his porch.

"You knew what old man?" Milya asked.

"I got your old man. Look at you, you're as pregnant as a billy goat."

"What?"

"You heard me. I can see it all in your face. You done gone and broke your leg."

"Uncle Bennie that's not true. I have seen evidence of my timely visitor. By the way, it's good to see you too."

Milya hugged and kissed him and walked pass him into her mother's house." Katie, Zaria and Reba were sitting at the kitchen table waiting on their arrival.

"What's up gang?" "Milya asked as they all greeted each other. "I must get me a glass of milk with ice. Does anyone else want something while I'm at the fridge?"

"No thanks," Reba said." But come and sit down and tell us what's wrong. You know you are not good at hiding things from me, and your drinking milk with ice is a sure sign that you have something to say."

"Well guys, I have been extremely moody lately."

"Whoa, that's one of the early signs girl," Katie mentioned.

"I haven't missed any periods."

"That don't mean a thing girl. Your aunt's cycle had to be stopped by the doctor well over into her pregnancy. That didn't mean she wasn't with child."

"But I haven't missed any pills." Milya stopped talking and placed her hand over her mouth, then said, "Oh my GOD. When I think about it, there could be a slight possibility."

"I'm sure there is one," Zaria said with a big grin on her face.

"Ok, let's go to the grocery store and pick up a few extra items. We will also choose one of those early home pregnancy tests. We'll definitely know before the night is over," Reba suggested.

The ladies took Reba's car, which was parked at the back of the house, and went to the store. They wanted to go and return before the men knew they were gone.

Stan thought he heard a car leave. He looked around and saw Reba's tail lights pulling out of the back drive.

"Guys, they're leaving without a word. Couldn't this get a little tricky?" Steven said looking a little worried.

"Steven, that may be a good thing. They may still be out when the show down takes place. I, for one, am all for that. We will have to keep an eye out for their return." Rick stated.

Just as Rick had imagined, Big Dee had his men in place. He was going to teach his brother a lesson without getting the police involved. Gangs had a way of dealing with their own.

Rick and Steven sat with Uncle Bennie on his garret. They saw the car as it slowly approached the house. Actually, there were two cars filled to capacity. They threw smoke bombs and got out of the vehicles ready for battle. What they were not ready for was the sight of Big Dee.

He had them surrounded. He walked towards Frank and said, "Hi little brother; tell your men to drop their weapons."

Frank didn't argue. He did what he was told. Bethany on the

other hand was so set on revenge until she tried to take action by herself. She charged at Big Dee like a run-away train. He nearly broke her in half. When she fell this time, she didn't move again.

Big Dee looked at his brother and said, "It's a shame that you let a little piece of tail come between us."

"Dee, Dee, it's not like that," Frank interrupted.

"Stop lying." Big Dee said before he struck Frank in the mouth, loosening a couple of his teeth.

Big Dee gave instructions to the men he brought with him to take care of everyone. He then went up to Rick, who along with the others, was still sitting down watching the action.

"Thanks again for obtaining this much needed information. It's good to know you still have friends who really care."

"Now you know I was looking out for my best interest." Both men laughed.

"I can promise you this, after this little escapade, Frank will think four times before he does anything else like this again. You know we take care of our own and by our own rules." Big Dee said shaking his head. "We will have this little matter cleaned up in about two minutes so that y'all can continue to enjoy your stay. See Ya."

He turned and walked away into the smoked filled area and disappeared the same way he arrived.

Milya and the girls made it back to the house. They parked in the rear as they normally did. Carrying their purchases, they entered through the back door.

"Milya," Reba said, "You run on along and check out your little situation."

"Yeah girl, we are so anxious." Katie said.

Zaria gave her an encouraging hug before she went to her room to administer the Maxell pregnancy test.

Uncle Bennie, Steven and Rick came in the front door with bags of their own. Rick pulled out bottles of champagne, and passed them around, along with cheese and crackers.

"Where's Milya?" He asked after he noticed she was missing.

"She's in the back. She'll be out in a minute," Reba stated.

"What's going on and why are we celebrating?" Katie asked.

"You'll see." Rick replied.

"Well you guys, I prepared some food earlier, and it will only take a few seconds to heat it up." Reba mentioned.

"Ms. Reba, you know that we can't resist anything you've prepared. My stomach is rumbling at the thought that you've fixed us a little something," Zaria declared.

As they all went about setting things up, Milya wandered into the kitchen looking confused at all of the commotion going on. Rick saw Milya standing inside the kitchen entrance. He sauntered toward her and took her by the arm, leading her to a vacant chair so that she could be seated.

"May I have everyone's attention please." He announced.

They all stopped and looked at him.

"I have something I would like to say." "Well dammit say it then. Don't thank I'm gonna stop eating to listen to ya," Uncle Bennie said.

Rick gave Uncle Bennie a stern look and proceeded to make his announcement. First, he pulled a small box out of his back pocket, opened it, and revealed a two-carat diamond marquise solitaire ring.

Kneeling down on one knee, Rick said, "Milya, I want to profess my love for you, to you, and before our loving and supportive friends and family. Will you stay with me for the rest of my days and nights by becoming my wife? It will truly be an honor. Marry me, please."

Every female in the house yelled with excitement, and tears of joy began to flow, not realizing that Milya had not yet given her response. Rick leaned forward and kissed her firmly on her lips, while wiping a stray tear from her cheeks.

"Hell, I don't know why y'all so happy, that gal ain't said nothing yet. I wanna hear an answer." Uncle Bennie protested.

All eyes were on her, but she only had eyes for Rick. The look she gave was for his eyes only. "Yes, I accept your proposal," she finally answered.

Uncle Bennie said, "Well then, let's eat, drank and be merry." Everyone laughed and did just that.

Rick had reserved a hotel room for the two of them that night. After a lengthy session of love making, they lay together in each other's arm. They talked of their past, present and future.

By the time they left to return to the Delta, Rick had received the blood test result from the lab that he took. He was not the father of the other child as Milya had originally suspected. She had been somewhat reluctant to discuss children with him, since the idea of his possibly having an outside child nearly drove them apart.

"Milya." "Hmm."

"I have something to show you."

Rick reached into the nightstand drawer and produced the explanation form. It described his blood type as well as the child's. He gave it to her and watched her expression as she read it. She didn't give any indication as to what she was thinking.

Finally she said, "I'm glad that's all cleared up," as she folded the paper and handed it back to him.

They lay there a moment longer before Milya spoke.

"Rick."

"Yeah baby."

"I'm curious."

"About what?" He asked.

"What was all that about with Stan and Bethany? What did he have that was so important she would try to kill him for?"

"Oh honey, I forgot to fill you in."

"What?"

"Stan hid some jewels in your overnight bag."

"He did what!"

"He thought it was Zaria's. Well, let me tell the whole story so you won't be confused. To make a long story short, the diamonds had been stolen from one of the wealthiest families in the Delta, the

Franklins. They had old money on top of new money which makes for an interesting situation.

Anyway, the diamonds had been missing for a while. Frank and his gang somehow stumbled up on them, and then lost them.

In the meantime, Stan ran across the diamonds while uncovering some dirt on someone else. These diamonds were to be returned to the Franklin family.

Milya interrupted him. "Surely these are not the diamonds that the police have been looking for years. That burglary was all on the news."

"The one and only. You see, those diamonds were called Delta Heat. They were given that name by the Franklin's great, great grandfather, the late Mr. Larry Alonzo Franklin. Legend has it that he was a man to be feared. Supposedly, he carried those diamonds across the Delta in the scorching heat before the town was settled, and during a time when the country was rugged. At that time, not a man dead or alive tempted fate to get the diamonds and lived to tell their story. They became the most sought-after diamonds in the world.

"Oh I see. Thank you for sharing that story with me, but the only heat I'm interested in right now is the heat you gave me the last night we were at my mom's."

"Yeah right. I believe that's the heat that got you with child isn't it?" Milya looked surprised. She didn't realize he suspected anything.

"Don't look at me like that. A man who pays attention to him woman knows when her body is going through a change," he said rubbing her and penetrating her at the same time. "My intent is to keep you with me all the days of our lives by any means necessary."

"Hm.., I could deal with that," Milya said as she realized that life with him would work out after all.

About the Author

Patricia Jackson possesses and has a great passion for romance novels. She enjoys writing and creating various characters for her readers. She is a native of what is known as "The Delta", Greenville, Mississippi, who is married and has two children. She and her family live in the Metro Jackson area.

Printed in the USA
CPSIA information can be obtained
at www.ICGtesting.com
LVHW090818170824
788329LV00001B/92